The Unexpected Choice

by

Stephanie Taylor

The Unexpected Choice
by Stephanie Taylor
Published by Astraea Press
www.astraeapress.com

This is a work of fiction. Names, places, characters, and events are fictitious in every regard. Any similarities to actual events and persons, living or dead, are purely coincidental. Any trademarks, service marks, product names, or named features are assumed to be the property of their respective owners, and are used only for reference. There is no implied endorsement if any of these terms are used. Except for review purposes, the reproduction of this book in whole or part, electronically or mechanically, constitutes a copyright violation.

THE UNEXPECTED CHOICE
Copyright © 2012 STEPHANIE TAYLOR
ISBN: 9781621353980
Cover Art Designed by AM Studio Designs

To my husband, Bryan Griffin who has taught me that love really is a choice and not just a feeling. Thank you for choosing to love me when I'm hard to love.

To my uncle, Ron Taylor, who believed in me more than I ever knew until the moment passed for me to be able to say thank you. I love you and miss you every day.

To my cousins, Alex and Elizabeth. I admire both of you for your strength and determination to always do what's right by others. We don't say it much, but I love you two beyond words.

To Opal, my newest friend and confidant. I've never met you in person, but you're my rock, my AP guru, and an amazing gal. Every time we tell fart jokes, I remember why you're so awesome. Even if you did make your kid throw up.

To all of you who are reading this book, may you always choose to love. I hope you enjoy reading this book as much I did writing it!

Other Books by Stephanie Taylor:

Lucky for Her
The Picture
Tinseltown
My One True Love
Doubting Thomas

CHAPTER ONE

STACEY OPENED the window to her grandfather's room to let out the stale air. After the years he'd spent smoking, the house still smelled pungent after a rainy day. She rested her head against the screen and inhaled the sweetness of the moist earth after a summer storm. Thunder still rumbled in the distance, giving the illusion of the sun chasing away the storm.

Stacey smiled and pushed her glasses up on her nose. "Are you okay, Papa?" she asked, straightening his covers and fluffing the sides of his pillow. He grunted and gave her a weak smile.

"I'm fine. Just tired, pun'kin," he rasped.

"Do you need some water? Is your throat dry?" Stacey reached for his cup, but his shaking hand stopped her.

"I'm fine. Go read or something, I'll call if I need you."

Stacey placed his hands back at his sides, and his eyes drifted close. At only sixty-five, his body was being ravaged by cancer, and the doctors had offered little hope. Combined with the fact he'd refused chemo treatment after learning it would only prolong the inevitable. Stacey had begged, pleaded with him to do something, but as a war veteran and Purple Heart recipient, he'd lived through plenty of pain.

She didn't blame him, but her heart hurt when she thought about the man who had raised her not being there anymore. Gazing into his aged face, she gave a wistful smile. His thin lips were pale and drawn. The white hair on his head had never seen a day of gray. The fragile frame of his rib cage rose and fell softly, his breath much more shallow than last week.

Hospice would be here for their daily visit soon enough. Stacey left him and went into the living room to tidy up.

A knock at the door startled her, and she looked out the window. With a smile, she opened it and said, "Hi, Joey!" Adjusting her glasses on her nose, she stepped aside. It wasn't often her neighbor's son came for a visit, and it set her heart to racing every time.

With a nod of his head, his lazy, confident gaze trailed over her as he stepped inside. "How are you, Stace?"

He wasn't the first one to shorten her name, but something about his southern drawl and the way his mouth quirked on the end of it caused her bones to feel like mush.

"I...I'm good, how are you? What brings you by?" She closed the door and turned to watch him cross the small living room.

"Mom said your granddad was getting sicker. Wanted to check on you and see how you're doing." He kept his back to her, and finally stopped at the edge of the couch.

"Me? Don't you mean Papa?" Stacey shook off the tenderness tugging at her heart, and her awkward, too-loud laugh filled the room.

"No," he said, finally turning to meet her gaze. "How are you, really?"

"I already said I'm fine." She tilted her head to the side, trying to read his strangely blank expression.

"I don't believe you." His cocked eyebrow irked her and she huffed. He might be one of the most confident men she knew, but he wasn't fooling her.

Stacey frowned. "Why not?"

"You're only twenty, honey. You've got to

be exhausted here with no one to help you. You've got dark circles under your eyes, and you still haven't gotten the stem on your glasses fixed. Duct tape won't hold forever."

Stacey felt the heat in her cheeks, and she absently touched her glasses. She knew she wasn't anything to look at, and it was kind for a man like Joey to even notice she looked worse than normal. "I'll get them fixed eventually. I'm not worried about myself right now. I just want to keep Papa as comfortable as possible. There'll be plenty of time for me after…"

In an instant, Joey was in front of her, taking her shoulders in his strong hands and squeezing. "Stacey, I'm worried about you."

"Because I haven't fixed my glasses?"

"Because you never smile anymore."

"I smile plenty, Joey McCrary." For her sanity, she moved away from his heat and those intense brown eyes that seemed to care. "Why don't you go back across the street and be with your parents? Take it from me, you should enjoy what time you have left with them."

"I want to help you," he said softly, as if she'd never spoken.

Taking a deep breath, she turned and gave him her best smile. "I don't need your help. Papa only has a little time left, and I won't let you come in here and take it away from me." Tears welled in her eyes until Joey was a blurred image. She felt his tender arms come around her and she accepted his embrace for only a moment. Being so close to him elicited selfish feelings, and she'd just read a passage in her Bible about that earlier today. Papa came first.

"Stacey?" she heard her frail grandfather call out.

She pushed away from Joey and he took a step back, but as she walked away, he grabbed her hand, causing her progress to stop.

"He needs me," she protested.

"Let me. I'm not a stranger to him, Stace. I mowed his yard every summer for six years. Sometimes a man needs another man for support. Having to bare everything to you is probably embarrassing to him."

Stacey swallowed thickly. She'd never thought of it in those terms. Leave it to Joey, childhood friend, to give it to her straight.

Once again, tears welled.

Tenderly, Joey tucked a strand of her curly hair behind her ear. "I'm not saying it to upset you, Stace. Just sit down and let me handle things, just for a little while."

"Why?" The word escaped before she could stop it. She suddenly felt foolish for questioning his good, albeit stubborn, heart.

His eyes grew soft and she recognized the look of pity. She hated that look but she couldn't stop it. In the small town they lived in, everyone knew practically everyone. Pity was part of it.

Poor little Stacey Ingram, gave up her education for her grandfather. Poor Stacey, such a kind soul to help him out. She'd forgotten how to live, poor thing.

Narrowing her eyes, she lifted her chin a notch, silently daring him to say anything even resembling pity.

"Why?" she asked again through gritted teeth.

Joey lifted a shoulder in a careless shrug. "Because you're my friend."

JOSEPH MCCRARY wanted a lot more than friendship with Stacey, but now wasn't the time. Right now, all she needed was his help. And all he needed was to see her smile again.

He was home for a while now since he'd graduated from college last week with a bachelor's in engineering. He'd planned to spend the summer interviewing for jobs and living up his last carefree summer before becoming an official adult with a nine-to-five job.

Until his parents had told him about Mr. Ingram and the cancer. His first thought had been to ask about Stacey, but his parents knew him well, and it didn't even pass his lips before they told him about how she dropped out of high school her senior year two years ago and wouldn't even speak to anyone about going back.

Over the years, he'd look to Stacey as a solid rock in his crazy world. He lived fast and free and didn't think much about the consequences. He enjoyed easy women and no commitment.

They'd grown up across the street from each other, building the cliché mud pies and swimming in the local watering hole. But she'd always been the awkward girl with knobby knees, thick glasses and frizzy blonde hair.

But something changed around the time he went to college. She'd been sixteen at the time and started filling out those baggy shirts she always wore, and her hair was less frizzy and more…tousled. Sort of like what he envisioned her looking like after a good roll in the hay.

But Stacey Ingram wasn't built that way. She was a forever kind of gal, one he'd normally steer clear of, but after the conversation with his parents about how out of touch with society she was, Joey had realized the perfect escape for her.

Him.

With a hopeful smile tugging at his lips, he entered Mr. Ingram's room and took a good look at the man who used to be his employer.

"Hey Mr. Ingram, how ya feelin'?" He

spoke loud enough for the man to hear him and extended his hand.

He obviously recognized him immediately by the way his face lit up with an ashen smile. Joey took his hand and pumped, ignoring the weakness of the other man's grip.

"I'm glad you're here, son, I need to go to the bathroom. Can you help an old man get there?"

"That's why I'm here, sir. I wanted to let Stacey get some rest."

His words gave Mr. Ingram pause. His eyes glistened suspiciously. "Why thank you. Everyone seems to fuss over me but no one thinks about her. I'm just a man who's at the end of a well-lived life. Hers is just beginning."

"I'm home from college now, and I'll be over here as much as I can to help out," he assured the man, his heartstrings tugging. Joey pushed the feeling aside to help him out of bed.

Once he was settled again, Joey strolled back in to the living room and found Stacey sitting on the edge of the couch, tissue in hand, glasses lying duct-tape side up on the coffee table. She didn't notice his entrance, and he watched for a moment. She wasn't the kind of gal to show her emotions much, and it was like getting a glimpse inside of her soul.

Her face crumpled, and she buried it in the tissue, quietly sniffing and swiping at her nose and eyes. For a moment, Joey felt the tears welling in his own eyes for her sorrow. She was such a beautiful girl—woman now—and his arms physically ached to hold her. Friends hugged each other, right?

Silently crossing the room, he sat next to her and gathered her into his arms, loving the feel of her softness against him. Her stiff body was an indicator she didn't welcome his touch, but he was determined. If there was one thing she should know about him by now, it was that he got what he wanted. And he wanted her.

Turning her face up to meet his, he wiped away her tears with his thumb and kissed her forehead. "Stace," he whispered, the lump in his throat vicious and choking.

"Thank you," she said without a trace of emotion in her voice. She tried to move away from him, but he tightened his hold.

"When was the last time you let someone hold you when you cried? Or tell you it was going to be okay?"

She swallowed and averted her eyes. "Before Mama and Daddy died."

Joey inhaled a deep breath and let it out slowly. He remembered that night. The police cars, the sirens, and the flashing lights had called attention to the house he now sat in. He'd even heard Stacey's childhood cries through the closed window. She'd suffered so much, and yet she was so much stronger than anyone he'd ever known before. Maybe because of the things she'd endured over the years or despite them, he wasn't sure.

"You're beautiful," he murmured, touching her cheek.

Her eyes were wide and full of something akin to desire. It was a universal look for all women, but on her, it was special, knowing he caused it. He wasn't sure if forever was on the menu or if it was all just temporary, but he wanted to give her a glimmer of hope. Somehow make her see she still had a life to live.

"You're full of crap," she shot back with a half-smile and again tried to pull away.

"You think I'm kidding?" he asked, surprised she'd voice her insecurities.

"I know you are. Let go of me, Joey. I don't know what's wrong with you, but you need to go. I have to fix supper for Papa."

"You have to kiss me."

Her audible gasp caused him to shift uncomfortably in his seat. Was she horrified at the thought? Or was it the opposite?

She wrenched away from him, putting the whole expanse of the room between them with only a few awkward steps. She stumbled over the magazine rack at the door. "Joey McCrary, get out of this house or I'll…"

He grinned. "Or you'll what?"

Stamping her foot like the true southern belle she was, he tried not to laugh out loud.

"Wipe the smirk off your face," she ordered.

"Make me." It was fun getting her all flustered, seeing the life back in her eyes and color in her cheeks.

"Get out."

He crossed his arms and leaned back on the couch. "Nope."

"I'm gonna call your mama."

He tossed her a careless shrug. "Go ahead, but I'm bigger and faster than her these days."

That got a smile out of her. A real, genuine Stacey Ingram smile that had captivated him when he was younger. He was glad it still charmed him, even if it was disturbing to recognize now how she'd always affected him.

His heart stopped a little as her smile faded and the insecurities crossed her face, plain as day. She looked at her feet, and a pretty shade of pink rose on her cheeks.

Standing slowly, Joey walked to her. The thud of his shoe against the hardwood caught her attention and her gaze snapped up. His gaze travelled down her, lingering on her hips. The sexiest curve on a woman was right above those hips, and he loved to nibble on it.

He gave her time to back away, and he

recognized the fear in her rounded eyes. Her glasses were still on the table, probably why she'd stumbled. Her blindness gave him an advantage.

Walking right up to her, he invaded her personal space, waiting for her rejection, but those eyes were trained on his lips, and her own were open in a silent gasp.

"What are you doing?" she asked, her voice breathy and low.

"What does it look like I'm doing?"

"I'm afraid to say because if I'm wrong, I'm going to look like an idiot."

Joey chuckled. "You're not wrong." He reached up and tugged at a tendril of her blonde curls. The action brought her even closer to him. He took a step forward, forcing her body to back up until she touched the wall.

Stacey let out a little squeak.

He put his hand on her luscious hip and squeezed. She slapped him away quickly. But he was a patient man and put it back there as soon as he recovered from the sting. This time she didn't make him move. There was no denying she was attracted to him. And maybe it was a little too soon for her, but he needed to feel her lips against his. He needed to know he could take away her pain, if only for a little bit, maybe longer if his plan came to fruition. But kissing her was the only way he knew how to help her.

He began his descent, a smile lifting the corners of his mouth. He could practically hear her heartbeat thrumming through her veins, and it caused his own body to respond.

Then, at last, his lips touched hers. Slowly he worked his mouth over hers, not demanding anything, just enjoying flesh against flesh until she opened for him. He wondered by the stiff way she held herself if she'd ever been kissed before by anyone other than him. Gripping her hip tighter and cupping the back of her head with his other hand, he leaned into her, pressing himself against her.

Stacey squirmed and tried to say something, but he took her mouth the second it opened, her words lost. She relaxed then, so much so she clung to his shirt. He helped her out by moving her arms around his shoulders, pulling her tight against him and hanging on.

Tentatively, her tongue touched his, fueling his desire. Who knew little Stacey Ingram was so perfect? With a groan, Joey deepened the kiss, giving her everything he had, praying desperately if just for a moment, she was thinking of something other than her grandfather.

As she kissed him back, finally giving in, it didn't take much for him to realize he was in over his head. If Stacey had never been kissed before, she was a fast learner. Joey's thoughts were already turning to the bedroom, and that didn't typically happen this quickly for him. Yeah, he was a guy, and he considered himself experienced. The women blended together for him. But nothing about Stacey blended. She was kind, beautiful, and had the sweetest smile he'd ever seen.

It was those thoughts that had him pulling away. She followed him awkwardly, obviously unwilling for the moment to end, but he took her hands away from his shoulders and placed them in front of her.

Without letting on that his heart was pounding and the ground had quite literally shifted beneath him, he gave her his practiced, sexy grin he gave all the gals at college. "What time can I come over to help tomorrow?"

Her dazed eyes narrowed and finally focused on him. "Help me with what?"

His grin blossomed into a full smile. "Mission accomplished."

CHAPTER TWO

Sure enough, Joey showed up on her doorstep at exactly noon the next day. Since she'd never been kissed the way he'd kissed her the day before, Stacey had no idea how to act around him. Did she greet him with a smile? A hug? Another kiss?

Instead, she did none of those things. She called from the kitchen for him to come in, but in reality, she wished he'd go away. Joey wasn't the kind of guy she wanted to get involved with. In fact, she didn't want to get involved with anyone, period. She had things to look after and her grandfather to take care of. Why did everyone think it was such a waste of her time to take care of him?

Suddenly annoyed, Stacey turned at the sound of his heavy footsteps and wielded a spatula in his direction.

"Don't you come in here thinking you own the place today, Joey. You're forgetting I know all about you and how you play women. Your kiss was nothing but a distraction yesterday."

"And it worked, right?" He held his hands up as if she pointed a gun at him instead of a greasy cooking utensil.

"Don't play games with me." Her gaze narrowed on his innocent expression. "I'm no more your type than Papa's old LTD, so don't you think you're fooling anyone here."

Joey lifted his shoulder in a careless shrug. "I admit it, you're not my type. At all."

Stacey felt the heat in her cheeks and silently cursed. When would her body get the message she was an adult now? Turning back to the meat on the stove, she focused her energy on browning the meat instead of keeping Joey away. Her heart did a funny little jig in her chest when his strong arms wrapped around her and tried to take the spatula away.

She was no expert, but she was pretty sure the slow way he slid his palm down her arm was meant to turn her on. Jerking away, she shot him a glare, refusing to admit it worked.

"Get off me."

"Stacey," he whispered against her ear, causing her stomach muscles to clench. "Let me help you."

"I'm perfectly capable of cooking."

"I never said you weren't. That looks like some mean pasta, but I'm capable, too. And I want to help."

Defeated and desperate to be rid of his closeness, she dropped the spatula on the spoon rest and spun away from him.

His chuckle followed her and when she reached the door, she turned and stuck out her tongue at his back. He didn't see her, but she felt better anyway.

"I'll be getting Papa ready for lunch. Don't burn it."

As she entered Papa's bedroom, she smelled the stale odor of sweat and turned instead to draw water in order to bathe him. His spirits always seemed lifted after he freshened up.

Last night had been long, with him coughing and Stacey helping him up and down to use the bathroom, which was becoming increasingly painful. She'd had to administer morphine at dawn so he could settle and get some rest. But sleep had never come for her.

She was no expert, but common sense told her he didn't have much longer. The rattle in his chest from congestive heart failure was worse, and the doctor hadn't been able to get it under control with medication. With the exception of the previous night, he was pretty much always sleeping.

Stacey knew she shouldn't fuss so much over him. After all, a man had his pride. But she simply couldn't let him go yet. He was all she had left and maybe it made her selfish, but it just wasn't in her to let go so easily.

He slept through the entire bath, only muttering a few words. The morphine hadn't quite worn off yet, and she was grateful he slept so soundly. She let the tears fall freely as he slept. Every day it seemed his body grew more skeletal, more gaunt. His ribs were all prominent, and she could see the two gunshot wounds he'd gotten during his stint in the army as well as the pink puckered scars from his exploratory surgery right before his cancer diagnosis.

It was times like these Stacey wanted to be angry with God. What had her grandfather done to deserve such an end? He'd protected his country, been a good husband and father, and chased away all of her nightmares since her parents had died. What purpose did God have in doing this?

But even as Stacey found her anger swelling, she tempered it, because anger would get her nowhere. God *did* have a purpose, and she believed that. She just failed to see it and wasn't sure she'd ever be able to. There was so much unfairness in the world, but she recognized there were others in more dire situations than she or Papa.

There's always someone worse off than you, her mother used to always tell her.

Stacey poured out the water in the bathroom sink and wiped the evidence of her tears away. She could still hear Joey in the kitchen fumbling around. Whatever he was doing didn't smell like what she'd started for dinner. Her mouth watered, but she refused to go in there, knowing he'd be able to see she'd been crying.

Instead, she returned to Papa's room and raised the window. The birds were singing their summer melodies, and there wasn't a cloud in the sky. Shade from the huge oak tree out back lined the window like a huge umbrella, taking away all the heat and leaving only a cool, rustling breeze. For a moment, Stacey inhaled and lifted a silent prayer to the heavens.

God, give me strength to get through this.

JOEY WASN'T sure how to go about executing his plans for Stacey. His mother had told him about her need to be grounded, to be pulled back into reality. But he knew her well enough to know she'd never leave her grandfather's side. Not until he was gone.

The surprising thing was, he *wanted* to help her. Joey wasn't so self-absorbed he couldn't admit he was selfish, sometimes to a fault, but this time, he found himself looking at Stacey and longing to see a trace of the pretty girl he'd grown up with.

All he saw now was a too-thin, jittery and hostile woman who got her dander up about everything. Stress could do that, he knew. College had put him and stress on a first name basis. But he didn't want to have to provoke her into anger just to see the light back in her eyes. The question was now, could he be the person she needed?

It wasn't a secret Stacey had a crush on him while they were growing up. Of course, he'd been pretty stupid back then and hadn't paid much attention to the way she drew hearts in the mud or seemed lost in thought when he sat next to her with his fishing rod. But one thing was certain; Stacey was going to be his, in every way possible. He'd do whatever it took to make her see that.

"What are you...?" Stacey demanded as she rounded the corner.

She'd been crying again. He took a deep breath to keep his protective instincts from kicking in.

"*Voila*," he said with a smile. "I hope you like Italian."

She didn't so much as glance at the food he'd cooked. "I thought you were cooking what I had laid out."

"I never said I was."

"You lied to me."

"About what?" Carefully placing the spoon on the stove, he leaned against the refrigerator and tilted his head.

"You came here to make my cooking look bad."

Joey cleared his throat. The thought was so ludicrous, he couldn't even laugh. "Stace, c'mon."

"I don't need you coming in here, playing the knight in shining armor or whatever it is you're doing. We were doing just fine before you, and we'll do just fine without you. Now get out."

Her voice shook, and her eyes shone brightly behind her glasses. With a sniff, she pushed them higher on the bridge of her nose.

"I'm not leaving."

"Yes, you are. Or I'm calling the cops."

At that, he did laugh. "Sweetheart, I've been in a lot of hairy situations, but getting the cops called on me for cooking lunch for a friend is a bit ridiculous, don't you think?"

Stacey swallowed and bit her bottom lip. After a moment, she said, "Look, I appreciate what you're trying to do. Really. But I can't let you."

He took a step toward her. "Why are you really upset, Stace?"

Her face crumbled, and she threw her arms in the air. "Because, Joey! The food you cooked took up all of our groceries for the week, Papa had a bad night last night, I didn't sleep at all, and—"

Joey stopped her rambling with his fingers. "Are you guys having money trouble?"

"Of course we are, you idiot. He's got cancer. I don't work. The bills are adding up. I've been living off rice and beans for months now, but it's the only way I can keep up. Even then, it's not saying much if keeping up means I'm two months behind on every bill I owe."

Joey couldn't help himself this time. He swallowed the distance between them in two long strides and he pulled her into his arms. "I'm so sorry."

She pushed weakly at his chest. "Don't be. I don't want your pity."

"I don't feel sorry for you, Stacey. I just wish you didn't have to go through this. You're too young."

"Twenty kind of feels like two hundred these days."

Joey pulled back and tucked her unruly hair behind her ear. "That's why I'm here."

"Be honest with me. You've been gone two years, and I haven't seen you but a handful of times when you've been home from college. Why are you suddenly taking such an interest in my situation?"

"That's easy, Stace. Because I love you." When her brows came down in a fierce frown, he backpedaled. Maybe it wasn't the best thing to say, given the circumstances. "We're friends, right? Even while I was in college, I always thought about you. Wondered how you were doing. Mom gave me updates occasionally, but I still wondered. I wanted to see you for myself."

She pushed her glasses up on her nose again. "I think the lack of sleep is getting to me. None of this is adding up."

Good, it wasn't for him either. "Why did you quit school?"

"Same reason you *finished*." She gave him a careless shrug. "I wanted to."

"I don't believe it. You used to always talk about going to college."

"Things change. I changed. You can't take education with you when you die, Joey. It's different for a man, though. You'll have to provide for a family one day. I just want to be a wife and mother. The only education I need for that is the Bible."

He nodded, swallowing thickly. Was now the right time to ask what he'd come to ask? "You'll be a wonderful wife and mother." Slowly, he slid his palms up and down her arms, watching her lids droop at his touch.

She was too tired. Now certainly wasn't the time. "Are you hungry?" he questioned before placing a gentle kiss on her forehead.

"Just sleepy."

"Go lie down. I'll make sure Mr. Ingram gets fed, and I'll save a plate for when you wake up. I'm here for the rest of the day so take advantage of me."

Stacey raised an eyebrow at his words and he chuckled.

"That way, too, if you want, but you need to rest first. I like my women spunky."

The sweet pink he'd come to love rose in her cheeks, and he chuckled again. He turned her around in the direction of her room and patted her bottom.

He watched as she made her way to the door. Just before she rounded the corner, she glanced back at him and smiled.

"Thanks, Joey."

He tipped an invisible hat and winked. "My pleasure, ma'am."

Stacey came awake a little at a time. Just when she thought she was well-rested, she'd wake up again a while later. Occasionally she'd hear the murmurs in the living room, but she couldn't remember the last time she'd been able to ignore them.

Without warning, the door burst open. Sitting straight up, her eyes wide, she saw Joey standing in the door, breathing hard and sweat beaded on his brow.

Somehow, before he even said anything, she knew. "Papa!"

Throwing the covers back, she tumbled out of bed and pushed past Joey.

The hospice nurse sat at his side, administering something through an IV. "What's going on?"

"He's asking for you," Joey supplied behind her. "Jane here says it's almost time."

A sob choked Stacey's airway, and she walked past the nurse and sat on the edge of the bed. "Hey, Papa," she said. His smile was weak, and his shaking hand reached for her. He took her face and brought it down to his lips.

"I love you," he whispered.

"Oh, Papa," she said, swiping at the tears so her last vision of him wasn't blurry.

"Be good, punkin," he whispered. Slowly, his eyes found Joey, and he pointed his finger without moving his hand. "He loves you. Love him back." His breathing was ragged and slow. The hospice nurse gave Stacey one of those impersonal, sad smiles.

She felt Joey's hands on her shoulders and the gentle squeeze of reassurance. Amazement drifted through her at her grandfather's words. The morphine was talking; it had to be. A tear fell down her cheek. He must want to believe Stacey would fall in love with Joey and have a good life. If it would make him happy for him to believe that, she'd play along. Anything for his passing to be easier.

"I've always loved him, Papa," she said softly and placed her hand over his. "We'll be happy."

Joey squeezed her again. She barely felt it as she watched Papa draw what would be his final breath. His lungs rattled, and his lips were ashen. His eyes suddenly went distant, and Stacey knew his soul was gone. Her papa was dead. The man who'd willingly stepped up and become her father when her own wasn't there.

The tears choked her. She struggled for air, but she didn't care if she lived or died. Stacey had nothing left to live for. There was no job to distract her, no man and no friends. All of that had gone by the wayside the second Papa got sick.

"I'll call the funeral home when you're ready. Take all the time you need," the nurse said quietly as she made some final notes on her chart and checked Papa's pulse. She didn't have to feel for herself to know it wasn't there. His chest was no longer moving, his mouth had gone slack, and his eyes, while opened, held no hint of the life he'd lived so well.

The room spun as she stood up. This couldn't be her final memory of him. She didn't want to remember him this way, so lifeless and…dead.

She felt the warmth of Joey's arms wrap around her, but she freed herself. Stars spotted her vision, and somehow Joey turned her to face him. His hands came up to rest underneath her jaw.

"Breathe, baby," he whispered, his eyes bright. His words trembled. It was all Stacey needed. Letting out a howl of despair, she sank to the floor, taking Joey with her.

"Papa!" she cried out, her heartache digging so deep tears didn't even well. The hole in her chest ached, and she gripped for a solid surface. Joey was the closest thing.

Tenderly, he gathered her on his lap and held her close.

What was she going to do without her Papa?

Joey stifled his own sadness, which he knew was so small in comparison to Stacey's. Mr. Ingram had been a great man. And his prophetic words before his death resonated in his mind.

He loves you.

Yes, he did love her, but not the way the man wanted to believe. Stacey Ingram was a beautiful, sensual girl, and he intended to marry her, but loving her wasn't part of his plan. At least, not right away. Maybe someday his heart would melt a little for him to feel something more than friendship for another woman.

Scooping her limp form into his arms, he moved to the bedroom and put her on her bed. She had cried herself to sleep on the floor of her grandfather's room.

Joey made sure she wasn't going to budge and went back out to give the nurse some instructions for the funeral home. After everything was settled about an hour later, he lay down beside Stacey and held on. She'd need someone when she woke up. He might not be who she wanted, but he wouldn't go down without a fight.

The funeral home director came and went. He was glad Stacey didn't have to see her Papa's body being taken away. The nurse peeked her head in the door and told him she left some paperwork and numbers for counseling and let herself out quietly.

He wasn't sure how long Stacey would sleep, but he didn't intend to leave her side until he was certain she would be okay. The painful cries from her loss had been enough to bring him to his knees, literally. For a twenty year old, she'd seen too much, been through far too many things in her short lifetime. Joey wasn't about to let her go through the rest of her life like a statue.

He was going to make her have fun. Feel. Live.

But for now, his plan would have to wait.

CHAPTER THREE

AT ONE POINT during Papa's illness, Stacey had thought she'd feel relief when his suffering was over. In a way, she was glad he was now with her parents. What a beautiful reunion it must have been! She could just see the tears of joy on her mother's face and the firm handshake her dad would have offered the second Papa was within reach.

Stacey sighed. But there was the selfish part of her. The part of her that wanted him there to help her through life, to guide her. Even though the house was small, it swallowed her now that she was alone. The silence deafened her at times. She found she didn't want to be alone.

Joey was steadfast during the day, keeping her company, urging her to go out and keep her mind off things. But what he didn't understand was she wasn't ready. Papa's life deserved to be remembered, honored, and she just couldn't bring herself to go on like he'd never been such a major part of her world.

At night, when Joey walked across the street, she was still alone. Still afraid of what her future held. She realized selfishness had sunk deep claws in her. Papa would have never wanted her to act this way. In fact, hewould have scolded her and told her to get her heart off her sleeve and get back to being a kid.

Trouble was, she'd never been a kid. She didn't know how to be young and carefree. Joey asked her out several times, but she couldn't face the fact it was a pity date. He'd seen her at her lowest and been there for her. He was simply trying to follow through. It was an admirable trait, but not one she could abuse.

A few days after the funeral, Joey started his new job as an engineer. She was excited to see him pull into her driveway at precisely fifteen minutes after five and stroll up to her front door wearing his suit.

"Don't you look handsome?" she asked with as much enthusiasm as she could muster.

"I've been called worse," he said with a grin and stepped in without invitation.

"How did your day go?"

He bent and kissed her forehead, like Stacey imagined a loving husband would after coming home from a long day at work. "Pretty good. Not much to do now except read stupid manuals. Gotta wait for my security clearance to go through."

Stacey took his jacket as he shrugged it off and loosened his tie. "How long will that take?"

"A couple of weeks."

She laid his jacket across the back of the chair, careful not to wrinkle it.

"What's for dinner?" he finally asked.

"Um, I..." Stacey hadn't thought that far ahead.

"Let's go out somewhere," he said before she could come up with something to cook out of the meager supplies in the fridge. He took her hands and cast pleading eyes on her.

"Joey..." she protested and walked past him.

"You can't stay in this house forever, Stace. At least let me treat you to dinner."

"You've been asking me every day since Papa died. I'm just not ready. I don't think I could handle everyone's pity."

"What if I threatened to beat them up?"

She couldn't help but smile. "You're sweet, but no. I'm not going anywhere."

He tossed a careless shrug and ambled over

to her. "Fine, then we'll order in. Maybe watch a movie or something tonight."

Through squinted eyes, she studied him. "I'm tired," she tried, just to see what he said. She had a strange suspicion something was up his sleeve. He had the same look in his eye he'd had when he sneaked off with Linnea Summers during third period at school their tenth grade year. He might have been bigger than his mama, but he hadn't been able to sit down for a week. Linnea had broken up with him eight days later.

"Then we'll go to bed," he said. He said it so slyly, so carelessly Stacey almost missed his meaning. After a double take, she pointed a finger at him.

"Get out."

"What?" he raised his hands innocently, like she might shoot him. Come to think of it, she just might.

"I'm grieving my grandfather's death, and you're trying to get laid. What's *wrong* with this picture, Joey? Get out of this house right now!" Stacey grabbed a newspaper from the coffee table and rolled it into a cylinder.

"You gonna club me to death?" he chuckled with a raised eyebrow.

Stacey popped his forearm with it, and he took a step back, surprise rounding his eyes. "That actually hurt."

"I learned a few things from Papa over the

years." She hit him again over the head.

"Stacey, don't make me fight back."

She didn't even bother with a reply; she whacked him over the head as hard as she could again.

Without warning, he charged her like a linebacker, and her world tilted over his shoulder. "Put me down, you're going to ruin your suit!" Stacey smacked him on the butt, and he laughed.

"Not a chance!"

She didn't want to laugh. Really she didn't. In fact, she was pretty sure the bubble of giggles turning into muscle-tensing belly laughs was a reaction to all the stress and sadness in her life. But she couldn't stop it any more than she could stop the world from turning.

His laughter joined her as he settled her back on the floor. Together, they laughed for what seemed like ages before their eyes collided, and Joey's thumb came up to outline her jaw.

"You're beautiful, Stacey. I don't know how I missed it before."

Sobering quickly, she looked away. "That's easy. There's not a hundred and twenty-six other girls fawning over you in my living room like they were in high school."

"No one is fawning, actually. And it's a nice change. I can be myself around you." Joey took a step toward her.

There was that feeling again. The feeling she wasn't going to like, or rather, like too much, what he was about to say or do.

"I want you, Stacey. I know it's not the right time, but I'd like you to give this a chance."

His simple declaration caused a spear of desire to go through her. She tried to imagine the statement wasn't finished, and he instead meant *I want you, Stacey, to fix some dinner*. Men like Joey McCrary didn't like girls like her. Mousy and quiet with the cliché duct tape holding up her glasses.

"What would you like me to order for dinner?" Instead of answering the peculiar look in his eyes, almost like he was surprising himself, she forged ahead and pretended not to hear him.

Joey cleared his throat. "Stacey."

Panic shot through her, and adrenaline caused her heart to race. No, no. She wouldn't acknowledge the real meaning behind what he'd just said. Turning, she inspected the contents in the drawer behind her where she'd last seen the take-out menus.

"Let's see, I've got a Chinese takeout, Japanese, Mexican. What do you feel like?"

As she rifled through the drawer for the menus, Joey's warmth surrounded her. His strong hand came around and grabbed her wrist, forcing her to turn.

Joey's lips descended. Stacey could feel his breath, hot and soft against her own. Just when she felt the slight touch of his mouth to hers, his lips slid across her cheek and back to her ear. "I'm a patient man, Stacey. One day soon, very soon, I'm going to make love to you." His teeth nipped her earlobe, and she was afraid the moan she just heard came from her own throat.

"I won't sleep with anyone unless I'm married to them."

Joey pulled back and smiled at her. The smile was so brilliant it had to be forced.

Standing on her toes, she put her lips to his ear and whispered, "Get used to disappointment, Joe."

She may have won the battle, but from the triumphant gleam in his eyes as she pulled away, the war was far from over.

STACEY DIDN'T know it, but she was playing right into Joey's hands. She needed someone with lots of patience, and he needed a wife. He thought about asking her then and there, but she deserved a more romantic setting and a little more time to grieve her grandfather. He'd eventually wear her down enough to agree to dinner, and then he'd pop the question when she was good and ready. Now he was just wondering if *he* would be ready.

"That was delicious," he complimented as he set his plate down on the coffee table. She took a deep breath and offered him one of those plastic smiles he'd come to loathe.

Stacey yawned and glanced at her watch pointedly. He had to admit, it was refreshing to have a woman not falling head over heels and begging him to stay.

"You're going to be tired for work tomorrow," she said, cocking an eyebrow.

"It's not even nine o'clock yet. Are you kicking me out?"

"Yes. I'd like to be alone. I haven't read my Bible today."

Joey studied her, wondering who she was when he wasn't there. "Do you read it a lot?"

Stacey primly folded her hands in her lap and looked down at them. "Some days it's the only thing that gets me to the next."

He reached out his hand and enclosed it around hers. "Don't I help a little bit?"

"Of course. But when I'm around you, I forget who I am, and I don't like that." Absently, she pushed her glasses up on her nose.

He tried to resist the urge to smile, but he couldn't. She was too cute. "Do you really know who you are, Stacey?"

She swallowed deeply, and her brows came together in a fierce frown. "I thought I did. And I know you're just being kind to me and this…attraction isn't real. We used to be friends, and I still think we are. But you don't have to keep up the charade. Papa's been gone for over a month now. Every day is hard, but it doesn't mean I can't cope. I'm not a little kid you have to keep checking on."

"I never said you were." Irritation gnawed at his gut. She truly had no idea how bright and beautiful she was.

"Why do you keep coming by? Acting like we're…a couple? Telling me things I know aren't true." A pretty blush rose on her cheeks. He scooted closer to her and allowed his fingertips to trace the pink marring her porcelain skin.

"Do you want to know who I think you are?" he said.

She frowned again and shook her head. "You're just going to make up things."

"Are you calling me a liar before I've even told you?"

Stacey tried to stand, but he tugged her back down, causing her to land across his lap. Exactly where he wanted her.

"Let go," she warned.

"I think you're a beautiful woman."

She rolled her eyes and shoved weakly at his chest.

"I think you've been through too much over the years to fully understand how it's impacted you."

"Pity. That's great." She shoved a little harder, but his grasp didn't relent.

"It's not pity, it's the truth. But I'm an outsider. I see you through honest, unjaded eyes, Stace. Yeah, what you've gone through is awful, but you're free now. What are you going to do with the rest of your life?"

Her deep breath gave away her annoyance. "I'm still too sad. I'm not ready to jump head first into relationships and life-long decisions. You've never lost anyone close to you. You've never gone through the emotions and wishing it was you instead of them." By the time she was finished, her voice trembled and her eyes glistened.

He swallowed thickly, trying to keep his head on straight. "I think you're wrong, Stace. Read your Bible. *All things work together for good for those who love Him.* You may not see it, but you've been surrounded by death to teach you something. What if I have a part to play in this?"

"You read the Bible?"

He shrugged. "I've been known to."

"That's so unfair…" she said to herself.

He grinned again. "One less reason to hate

me?"

"I don't hate you. I just don't believe you."

"You don't believe someone could think you're beautiful?" He reached up and turned her face so she was forced to look at him.

"I look in the mirror every day, Joey. Why don't you just cut to the chase and tell me what you want?"

The despair in her eyes broke his heart. She was clearly set in her beliefs and there was little he could do to change her mind tonight.

"I've already told you what I want."

"I can't sleep with you, Joey. I'm not that kind of girl."

"Can we settle on a kiss?" Hope sprang eternal but was crushed when he noticed the subtle shake of her head.

"I think you should go." She stood forcefully, breaking his hold around her waist.

"I'm not leaving until I get a kiss."

Following her, Joey stood and sauntered over to her usual corner, the one across the living room she used to try to stay away from him. Only it never worked. Once again, he wrapped his arms around Stacey's slender waist. At least she wasn't slapping his hands away anymore. She was getting used to his touch.

"Please go," she whispered and turned her head to the side as his lips descended.

"Stace, I lie in bed at night thinking about you, about how it would feel to wake up next to you. To touch you and kiss you whenever I want—"

"Stop it!" With a mighty heave, she sent him sprawling across the living room floor. His head connected with the corner of the recliner, and he let out a string of mumbled words he wasn't even sure he understood.

"It's just all fancy words, Joey! Do you think I don't know that? You don't care anything about me. Maybe you've just set your sights on me for whatever reason, but I'm not gonna give in. I'm not going to sleep with you because I'm lonely, or because I've always loved you. I will *not* listen to your lies anymore. This is my heart you're messing with. By your own admission, I've been through a lot. Don't you think you owe it to me to stop this before I fall even harder? Before I start believing this is possible? I don't need you anymore, Joey. Thank you for being here for me and being my friend. But we both know this is as far as it goes."

Finally, her little speech ended, and she took a deep breath. He hadn't moved. In fact, he'd stopped breathing, too. He'd listened to everything up until she admitted she loved him. No woman had ever said those words to him with the intensity and sincerity that left her mouth. He knew Stacey well enough to realize those words hadn't come lightly.

If he took a step back, this was exactly where he wanted her. She loved him. And he intended to marry her. But her admission gave him pause. He wasn't out to hurt her. In fact, their marriage would benefit them both. And they were friends already, so it wouldn't be like marrying a complete stranger.

Joey continued to stare up at her.

"Are you okay?" she finally asked, taking a step further.

Joey swallowed, the sound a hollow *thunk* against the quiet room. It was beyond him to speak. So instead, he simply shook his head.

He was far from okay. He was pretty sure he would never be okay again.

CHAPTER FOUR

JOEY DIDN'T come by the next day after work, and Stacey felt the hollow emptiness threaten to swallow her. He was late getting home. She was sitting at the table trying to figure out which bills to pay when she saw his car pull in across the street at his parents' house. A couple of hours passed as she slaved over bill after bill.

She was lost in a pile of paperwork when the soft knock sounded at the door and Joey stepped through. The first thing she noticed was the bead of sweat across his brow and how his breathing was labored.

"Someone chasing you?"

"No, I…"

"I didn't think you were coming by tonight, Joey. And it's late."

"I don't even get a simple hello?" He ambled into the kitchen, pulling out a chair and turning it backwards, the casual action contradictory to his heavy gulps of air. He propped his arms across it, looking at her with his charming brown eyes.

But there was wildness in those eyes that frightened her. What was wrong with him? Was he drunk? Taking some sort of drugs? She'd never known him to do those things, but a lot of years had passed since their childhood.

"Why are you here, Joey? I haven't changed my mind about sleeping with you." She tried desperately to ignore him by writing another check.

Long moments passed and finally his panting slowed. Absently, he picked up a bill, and his eyes bulged. "What are these?"

"What do they look like?" she countered, losing her temper and snatching the paper out of his hand.

"These are bills? Stacey, you're four months behind on your mortgage."

"The man can read." The embarrassment consumed her as she thought of the foreclosure notice at the bottom of the stack. She had two weeks to pack and find another place. Leaving her childhood home behind would stink, but it had to be done.

Suddenly, Joey stood up. "Why didn't you tell me it was this bad?"

"Because it's none of your business. And you were too busy trying to have sex with me." She snatched another bill away from him and placed it out of his reach.

Joey studied her for a long moment. "I think we should get married."

Stacey's jaw dropped, and her eyes went wide. Then hysterical laughter bubbled up from her throat. "Joey, you're such an idiot!" She swiped the tears away as she laughed.

But Joey bent down and placed a hot, open-mouth kiss on her lips, effectively silencing her giggles. Without waiting for an invitation, his tongue plunged into her mouth, and his fierce groan tugged at her core. She didn't want to feel anything for him. She didn't want to fall for his charm. And it angered her that he thought he could waltz into her home, speak of marriage so carelessly, and try to get her in bed again.

Gathering all of her strength, she turned her head to break the kiss. But Joey's lips traveled across her jaw and down her throat, settling on her erratic pulse. "I feel what I do to you, Stacey. Say yes to me."

His mumbled words teased her, made her believe if only for a split second she could have it all. But then reality crashed down. Papa was gone. Her parents were gone. Now her home. She didn't trust herself, or anyone else for that matter. She wasn't sure what Joey's motives were, but she was certain it was more than he was letting on.

The chair screeched its warning as she pushed away from the table and put some space between them.

"I don't know what you've been doing since you got home, but if you're into drugs…"

"Drugs? Honey, the only drug I'm on is you."

She snorted at his corny line. Her amusement must have shown because he gave her a slight shrug. His face turned solemn. "Marry me, Stace. You said you loved me last night."

Crap. She'd hoped and prayed those words hadn't really made it past her tongue as she'd feared, but apparently they had. "I love you as a friend, Joe. Nothing more."

"We can build on that." His eyebrows rose, and he smiled slightly. Once again, she was confused.

"This is unfair. I plan to marry someone who loves me, too."

"Stacey, we have all the elements of a perfect marriage. We're friends. We've known each other since grade school. I can be myself around you, and you need financial help. All the money my parents saved for college is untouched. I got scholarships. I can have your mortgage caught up with a single check."

Stacey wasn't sure what was going on. She was more certain than ever Joey wasn't telling her everything. "What's in it for you?"

Joey's lips curled in a sexy grin, and his eyes trailed from her face down to her breasts. "You."

"So you'd pay my mortgage in order to have sex with me. Isn't that something called *prostitution*?" Incensed, she narrowed her eyes. "You really know how to make a lady feel special."

"No, Stace…it's coming out all wrong. This isn't how I planned it." He ran his palm down his face and sighed.

"Planned what?" He'd *planned* this?

He scooted the chair out of the way and took her hands in his. "Stacey, I think we've got something special going, and I have something important to ask you."

Stacey cocked an eyebrow. Then Joey went down on one knee. "No, get up." She tugged in vain to urge him to stand.

"Stacey Ingram, will you marry me?"

She knew her eyes were round and horrified. And they got bigger when Joey pulled out a black velvet box. Surely her eyes were fooling her. This couldn't be real. She was standing in front of him dressed in her duct-taped glasses, pajama pants, and T-shirt. The ring, which looked to be at least a solid one-carat diamond, belonged on a queen's finger, not hers.

"Get up, Joey. This is ridiculous."

"I asked you a question," he said, his tone flat.

"The answer is no."

With a snap, he closed the velvet box and stood up. "I won't stop asking."

"I won't stop saying no."

"Yes, you will."

ONE DAY SOON, Stacey was going to wake up and the life she was living would be nothing more than just a horrible nightmare. Papa would be in his den, watching old reruns of M.A.S.H. and smoking his pipe.

Stacey hadn't seen a single wink of sleep last night, thinking about Joey and his proposal. Had it really happened? The bills still scattered on the table told her it had, indeed, taken place. But why?

There was definitely more to this than Stacey understood. Since it was Saturday, and Joey's car was parked across the street, she called him and asked him to come over. For sanity's sake, she had to get to the bottom of this. When he bounded up the steps less than five minutes later with an ear-to-ear grin on his face, her heart sank.

"Change your mind already?" He leaned in to kiss her, his eyes hot, but Stacey placed her hand over his puckered lips and directed him to the couch.

"Sit."

Surprisingly, Joey didn't argue. Stacey took a seat next to him. Draping a casual arm over her shoulders, he pulled her close to him and squeezed. An awkwardness settled between them, the embrace feeling more like a hug she might give a distant relative at a family reunion.

It took her a moment, but Stacey finally spoke. "I want the truth."

"I've given you the truth. I want to marry you."

"There's more to it. Stop lying to me. Isn't a marriage built on trust?"

"Is that a yes?"

Frustration gnawed at her and she stood up. She began her usual pacing when she needed to think. "No, it's not a yes." Shaking her head at her confusion, she then narrowed her gaze on him. "There's a reason behind you wanting to marry me. If there wasn't, you'd pick someone far prettier and far more social to do the job. Now spill it, McCrary." With crossed arms, Stacey stared him down with squinted eyes.

Obviously uncomfortable with her scrutiny, he shifted and then gazed across the room. "It's complicated," he said softly.

Stacey wasn't sure if she should feel vindicated her assumptions were correct or cry because her own insecurities had just been validated. "How complicated?"

"Very complicated."

Her pacing resumed. Did she want to hear this? "Start from the beginning."

With the sound of the popping hardwood floors under his feet, he rose and looked out the window. "I'm not a good person, Stace."

She swallowed thickly. "Why do you say that?"

"In college. I made a lot of mistakes."

"Everyone makes mistakes."

He shook his head violently. "I don't need platitudes. Just listen if you want to hear what I have to say."

When she didn't say anything, he continued without a glance in her direction. "I fell in love. I fell so deep and so hard, I didn't see five minutes in front of me. I just lived in the moment and didn't care about anything other than her and school."

Now Stacey was pretty sure she didn't want to hear this. But like watching a train wreck, she couldn't make herself stop him.

"We slept together. A lot. Every time I saw her, and we didn't use protection. She swore to me I was her first, and I knew I was clean. I just can't tell you how much I cared about her. I was so blind to everything, Stacey. I explained away the track marks on her arms, and I didn't think anything of it when she wouldn't stay all night with me. She was like *my* personal drug."

Stacey shifted her weight from one foot to another and took a deep breath to calm her nerves.

"She got arrested one night after we had a nasty fight over marriage of all things." He snorted a derisive laugh. "I wanted her to marry me, and she insisted she would never be attached to one person for long."

With an aching heart, Stacey walked to him and took his hand in hers. He didn't pull away but instead looked down at her with such sorrow, she wasn't sure she'd ever feel whole again.

"I'm so sorry," she whispered, the knot in her throat vicious and unyielding.

A muscle in his jaw pulsed as he looked back out the window, clearly lost in his own memories. "She's pregnant, Stace. My baby is going to be born into the custody of the state if I don't straighten up."

"Wha…?"

"Somehow I got connected with her drug bust. I spent a few nights in jail until my parents hired a lawyer to straighten everything out. But I'm still being watched, and the judge told me I had to meet certain criteria before my baby can live with me."

Stacey didn't like where this was going. "A judge ordered you to get married?"

"No. But my baby needs a mother. And I need a wife. It's as simple as that."

"So why me?" Glutton for punishment she was, she had to know.

"Because I know you. I know you wouldn't hurt a fly, and you live right across the street from my parents, so they could help out when we need them to. We could be happy together and we're both attracted to each other. I can pay your bills, help you get things back on track. You could go to school, do whatever you've wanted to. In return, I just need someone to help me raise my kid."

"A marriage of convenience? Are those even legal?"

"Isn't that what most people have these days, being that the divorce rate is over forty percent?" He tossed a wry chuckle over his shoulder and went back to watching a squirrel gathering nuts just outside the window.

"How would a judge even believe you could fall in love and get married in such a short time? And how long ago did this happen? When is the baby due? What time frame are you working on?"

Another low chuckle sounded. "I'm not a liar, Stace. I'd tell him the truth about us if we did get married. And Cameron is due in less than two months. She was arrested about six months ago, right before I came home for the summer. Seems like the timing couldn't have been more perfect for everyone involved."

Stacey had doubts about that. "So what are the terms? I help you get your baby and then we divorce quietly?"

He shrugged and turned back to her. He settled in his palms on her shoulders and massaged. "I don't know. I haven't thought that far ahead."

Joey looked so tired and different. She'd never seen him so dejected and lost. He'd once said he could be himself around her, so was this the real Joey she was seeing right now?

"I don't believe in divorce," she whispered, her eyes suddenly stinging as tears rose to the surface.

"I didn't either until I had a kid who needed me. Right now, my beliefs take the backburner."

"Don't you want to fall in love again instead of settling?" The tears fell against her cheeks and slid down slowly.

Joey's sharp gaze zeroed in on Stacey and he bared his teeth. "Oh, Stace. Such an optimist. Love isn't real the way we want to believe, honey. The only real thing is the pain."

"If there wasn't love, how could you feel pain?"

"Illusion. It's all an illusion."

Confused, Stacey pulled away from him and sat on the couch. After a moment, he joined her.

"You told me you loved me right after Papa died. I know you were trying to comfort me, but if you don't believe love exists, why say it?"

"I do love you. I love you as a friend and as a neighbor. But the gut-wrenching, lay-yourself-down-in-front-of-a-bus for someone is just hogwash. To me, what we have is far better than what I felt for Cameron."

Stacey disagreed, but she kept her mouth shut.

"Will you help me?" he asked next to her, his voice trembling and his hands shaking as he gripped hers.

"I don't believe in divorce," she stated again.

"We don't have to divorce."

"What if I fall in love with someone? How is any of this fair to me?"

"It's not. I admit it. It's not. But knowing

my own flesh and blood is about to be stuck in a foster home makes a man think twice about fairness. I'm just focused on getting my baby right now. The rest I can work out later."

Stacey fell silent again. But a single question floated through her mind and eventually worked its way to the surface. "Didn't you get yourself in trouble before when you didn't think things through?"

Abruptly, Joey stood and towered over her. "Will you help me or not?"

Charged with a confidence she'd never felt before, Stacey stood practically nose-to-nose with him. "I don't believe in divorce. I intend to be married to a man who loves me as much as I love him, even if it hurts sometimes. If you want to find a way for me to help without marriage being involved, I'll gladly do whatever you need me to. But I can't end the one dream I've always had, however impossible it might be, to find someone who loves me in a lay-down-in-front-of-a-bus kind of way. It does exist, Joey. I know it does. You know it, too, or you wouldn't be fighting so hard to ignore it."

"I never knew you to be so selfish, Stacey," Joey said as he ran a hand down his weary face.

"And I never knew you to be such a coward." Without stopping to think on her actions, she moved to the front door and held it open for him. He stopped in front of her and tilted her chin up with his index finger, forcing her to look at him.

With dead eyes and a determined etch to his lips, he said, "If you won't help me, I'll find someone who will."

CHAPTER FIVE

JOEY WASN'T sure what to do. The more he thought about it, the guiltier he felt for even bringing his situation to Stacey's attention. But he couldn't shake the feeling she would make the perfect mother to his child, and they could one day live a nice life together.

But it didn't stop him from thinking about her beliefs. He didn't want her doing anything she wasn't comfortable with. Knowing a wife had certain...duties to her husband was a little too much for him to take in, and he couldn't be sure he wouldn't ask more of her if they were married. A marriage of convenience could quickly turn into a marriage of demands. The physical attraction he felt for Stacey was gigantic compared to anything he'd ever felt, even with Cameron.

With Cameron, he'd felt an emotional attachment. He'd fallen into the trap people called love, which he'd discovered soon enough was a farce. With Stacey, it was just different. It was hard for him to put a name to what he felt for her, but he knew it wasn't just lust. But it wasn't love either. He was certainly attracted her, as well. A fact which had taken him by surprise. She might have duct tape on her glasses and wear shapeless clothes fit for a grandma, but the few times he'd held her and touched her, he knew she was anything *but* shapeless.

Which brought him back to his original problem. He couldn't ask her to do something that went against her beliefs. He was a cad; he admitted it. He'd slept around too much during college, made the wrong decisions and was now paying the price for it. Should he make Stacey pay for his sins, too?

Shame filled him when he thought about the tough times drawing him closer to God. He wasn't an overly religious man, but these last six months had brought him to his knees and his eyes to his Bible. And he respected the fact Stacey was a devout Christian. Truth be told, he didn't really believe in divorce either, especially after reading so much of the scriptures, but as he'd told Stacey last night, he was left with no other option. His lawyer had advised him to get his life right and find a steady income and a hobby.

Only by hobby, his lawyer meant wife. He'd never come right out and said it, but the undertones had certainly left little to the imagination.

Shame also filled him at the thought he'd let his attraction to Stacey get out of hand. Several times now he'd mauled her and said things to make her blush. Again, the attraction thing was bound to get out of control if they were married.

Filled with resolution, he crossed the street for the second time that day. He needed to apologize and tell Stacey how sorry he was for everything.

His hand was poised to knock, but the door flew open before he had a chance. Her hair was a rumpled heap on top of her head and her eyes were puffy. Tear stains on her cheeks caused his stomach to lurch.

"Stace…" he muttered and pulled her into his arms. "I'm so sorry."

Her somberness scared him a little. He pulled back to look at her, but nothing in her face revealed her feelings.

"I'm sorry, Stacey. I shouldn't have

involved you with my problems. You just lost your grandfather and here I am trying to convince you to marry me. Hardly fair, huh?"

"I'll marry you, Joey. But I have conditions."

Joey's heart stopped then started again with a great thump against his chest. "What?"

"I said I'll marry you."

"I can't ask that of you, Stace. I took advantage, and I shouldn't have."

"No, you're right. You shouldn't have. But you did. And I'm saying yes."

He stooped and looked into her eyes, which bore a hole through his chest. "Why?"

"I was orphaned once, when my parents died. And I know how important it is to stay with family. I'd like to help your baby."

He noted how she didn't say she'd like to help him, which clued him in she still had her reservations.

"What about your beliefs on divorce?"

"That's one of my conditions. No divorce."

Joey stood speechless for a second. "What do you mean, no divorce?"

"It might be a marriage of convenience, but if you're so convinced we're the perfect equation for a happy life together, then prove it. No divorce. Ever."

"I...I can't promise that."

"You said you weren't a liar, Joey. If you

stand before me, a preacher, and God and promise things you never intend to keep, you're a liar."

She had a point. So what reason would he ever have to divorce? If one of them fell in love, maybe. But it wouldn't be him.

"What if you meet someone you fall in love with? You were right last night. I can't keep you from your life. This isn't fair." He released her, torn between his obligations to do right for everyone involved in this mess.

"I won't fall in love with anyone, Joe. I guess we're a lot alike with things like this. People don't love girls like me."

From most girls, he might have thought it was a ploy for attention, but the dejected look on Stacey's face told him she truly believed the words.

In an instant, she was in his arms. He wasn't sure how she got there so quickly again, but he did know it was all his doing. The one thing he wanted to do for Stacey was protect her from herself. Once they were married, he'd make sure she had the confidence she needed to get on with her life.

With or without him.

STACEY TRIED to pull away from Joey, but his

grip was too tight. So instead, she inhaled his scent, outdoorsy and comforting. In a way, it reminded her of Papa.

It was easy to believe a life with Joey could be good. He always seemed to do the right things, say the right things, hold her the right way…But marriage was the tie that seemed to break a couple's perfect relationship. Once she was married to Joey, she held no illusion things would stay the same as they were now. He'd have what he wanted.

And at this particular moment, helping him was what she wanted. Helping a child know its father and having a chance to become a mother herself was what she needed. She was best at taking care of people, and an infant could certainly take her mind off her own woes.

"Joey…" She pushed at his chest. She didn't want his pity.

"Don't let go yet," he murmured in her ear.

"This isn't the part where you tell me how happy I've made you. I'm not stupid."

"I wasn't going to say that."

"And this isn't the part where you kiss me and take me to bed for us to celebrate." A knot formed in Stacey's throat, and she shoved it down with a thick swallow. What she said was exactly what she'd always envisioned.

"I wasn't going to do that."

"And this isn't the part where you lie to me

and tell me you love me."

"I wasn't going to."

Nope. Stacey was going to fight the tears. *Think of the baby.* The sweet baby she'd be able to raise.

"What were you going to do then?" she demanded, lifting her chin and shrugging out of Joey's arms.

For a moment, she thought Joey was going to cry, too. His eyes grew suspiciously bright just before he looked away.

"I was going to say thank you, Stacey." His eyes settled on hers again, clear and focused. "Thank you."

It was all that needed to be said. With a nod, Stacey stepped to the door and opened it, fingering her glasses up on her nose with the other hand.

Just as Stacey thought she'd be free of him for a little while, he paused just in front of her. "How do you want to do this? Courthouse? Justice of the peace? Small ceremony? Vegas?" She heard the smile in his voice but kept her eyes averted. Fear consumed her that if she looked at him, she'd get cold feet.

"No to Vegas," she said. Then she shrugged. "What if we just had something simple here in my back yard?"

"Perfect," he whispered. She watched in horror as his hand rose and nudged her chin upward. Somewhere along the way she closed her eyes, unable and unwilling to look at him. His soft lips, a simple pressing of flesh together and the tender swipe of his thumb against her cheek, left her reeling. They had to set some ground rules before they pulled the trigger.

Stacey opened her eyes and took a deep breath, ready to tell him what she was thinking.

But he was already gone.

COLD FEET. Joey could explain away his thought process by telling everyone he had cold feet. His mother might have loved the idea of Stacey and him getting married, but the more he thought about it, the more *real* it became. He was going to have a wife in a matter of hours. And he was going to be a husband. With responsibility. And in a few weeks, he would add father to the growing list.

He wasn't ready. No amount of preparation, reading *Mars and Venus*, or even praying about it was going to help him.

The fact was Stacey Ingram scared the wits out of him. Not because she was going to be his wife, but she seemed to reside in the little corner of his heart that hadn't been wrapped in the chains he'd carefully constructed after Cameron. He didn't love Stacey, doubted he ever would, but she made him feel.

And feeling again terrified him.

Even if it was a feeling that wasn't altogether unpleasant. Stacey didn't expect anything from him, which was refreshing, but he sure did owe her a lot. He didn't know another woman on the planet who would sacrifice her own happiness to help him get his baby. Except maybe his mom.

And *that* was something he refused to dwell on.

Inside the small room where he waited for the signal to go outside and meet his bride, he ran his fingers through his hair and paced. The room took exactly seven steps to get across. The ceiling had two water spots he'd need to take care of once they were back from their honeymoon. And there were thirty-nine books lining the shelves of the small bookcase, all romantic classics he knew Stacey favored.

His heart pounded, and he could hear the steady *whoosh* of the blood in his ears. What a mess he'd gotten himself into.

The last few weeks had blown by like a feather in hurricane winds. He'd worked, spent time with Stacey, paid bills he'd found statements for, and helped his mother plan a small ceremony in Stacey's backyard. Which was currently underway.

"It's time," his mother said softly from the

cracked door. "You ready?"

"Can one ever be ready for something so life changing?" he countered, straightening his tie and pulling at his jacket.

"I don't know, but we're about to find out." She entered the room and closed it with a quiet click. "Stacey is a beautiful girl. She's loved you since you two were little."

Joey wanted to argue, say Stacey had better sense than to love someone he was years ago. The truth was she barely knew him. But here she was, offering her entire life to him without anything in return. "I know, Mom. I just need to get through this without thinking too much. The last thing I want to do is hurt her. She deserves a lot more than what I can give her."

"Don't sell yourself so short, Joseph. You two are going to be just fine."

He wished he had his mother's confidence. He'd take a tenth of it, even.

She walked to him and placed her palm on his cheek. "You're all grown up now. You're about to be a father. Remember yourself. I raised you to always do the right thing. Go out there, look Stacey in the eyes and promise her you'll always be there and you'll always love her. You might think love is this overpowering feeling, but the reality is, years down the road, feelings eventually go away, and you're left with a choice. That's where you do the right thing. You *choose* to love her. Even if she wakes up looking like Medusa and has dragon breath, you remember what she's done for you and your baby today."

The lump in his throat dissolved as tears filled his eyes. "What about Cameron, Mom? As much as I never want to see her again, I can't stop thinking I'm going to hurt her by taking the baby. I loved her. A part of me still loves her. But I don't want to feel obligated anymore. I want to focus on Stacey, to try and make something of this, but Cameron keeps creeping back in when I least expect it."

His mother gave him a look he'd seen years ago when he'd cut his hair with a pair of school scissors. A mix between amusement and horror.

"Cameron made her choice, and it wasn't you," she said. Her smile softened the blow her words should have caused.

With a small nod, he walked to the door. She opened her arms, and he fell into them, leaning into the strength she gave him. He might have been a fool all these years to never listen to her, but he'd gotten his life all wrong because of it. Now, he was going to do what was right, make her proud and make Stacey proud to have him for a husband.

"Your daddy is walking Stacey down the aisle," his mother whispered. "And she looks beautiful."

Joey thought of her duct-taped glasses and gave a wry smile. "I can't wait to see her."

Even if she was wearing her customary pajamas, there was no way she could ever be anything but beautiful to him.

After walking down the aisle, he turned and looked out over the crowd. They'd both chosen not to have attendants in the wedding, so it was just him and the minister standing there. A crowd of about twenty-five people sat in the audience, all his family. Stacey had said she didn't have anyone to invite. The thought tugged at his heart. He had so many people to call family and friends. Stacey had only him. Another responsibility he was acquiring. He would literally be everything to her.

A moment later, his mother stood, as did the rest of the crowd. At the end, a girl in a white, modest dress stood on his father's arm. As he looked at her, he realized she actually wore a wedding dress. He wasn't sure how she'd come up with the money for it or where she'd gotten it, but she was a vision.

The dress hugged her curves up top, but revealed nothing but her shape. At the waist, the white dressed flared and fell down to the ground. The light from the sunset glistened off diamond earrings and an elaborate necklace draped around her neck. He recognized them from his mother's wedding photos.

In her hand, she carried a simple bouquet. He didn't know what kind of flowers were in it, but they were in typical fall colors. As his eyes rose to her face, she began to walk toward him. She tripped a little on her dress and shot his father an apologetic smile.

Then their eyes met. It was then he realized her glasses weren't on her face. Could she see him? The way she stared at him told him she could. Why didn't she always wear contacts?

Her hair was piled in loose curls on the top of her head, and little pearls were woven in. She was something, and at that moment, he felt like the luckiest man in the world.

But as his eyes settled once again on her, he saw the hesitation in her eyes in the way they darted just past him. A small blush pinked her cheeks, and finally her gaze fell to her bouquet and stayed there until she and her father reached him.

"Who gives this woman?" the minister asked.

"I do," his father announced and placed Stacey's hand in Joey's. Ice-cold fingers gripped him.

"Relax," Joey whispered with a smile as his father walked away and the crowd seated themselves.

"I can't."

Joey locked eyes with her and refused to let

her look away. He squeezed her hands and then rubbed them briskly with his thumb, trying to stimulate the blood flow again.

Finally, just as the audience quieted, he said, "You look beautiful, Stacey."

"Thank you."

But he could tell she didn't believe him. With another squeeze of her hand, he said it again, this time a little louder.

She grinned, another pretty blush creeping up her cheeks.

With a sigh, Joey resolved he'd have to make sure she believed him later. The minister cleared his throat, and Joey nodded for him to begin.

Within moments, a time frame Joey considered far too small to promise his life to someone, they were officially Mr. and Mrs.

"You can kiss your bride now, Joey."

Stacey was already practically glowing red by the time he turned to her, intent on sealing their deal with a kiss she wouldn't forget. But the terrified look in her eyes told him to treat her the way she deserved to be treated. With dignity and respect.

So he pressed his lips against hers and stayed there for a moment before pulling away.

As he did so, she touched her mouth with her fingers in true diva fashion to make sure he hadn't smeared her lipstick. He grinned. Her lips kicked upward, and she reached up to remove some of her lipstick from his mouth. Already acting like a wife. He liked it.

The thought caught him unaware, but the applauding crowd diverted his attention as the minister announced them.

Joey couldn't stop the smile spreading across his face anymore than he could stop the joy spreading in his heart.

CHAPTER SIX

Stacey McCrary.

Stacey McCrary.

Stacey *McCrary*.

Stacey stared at her reflection and tried to say the name out loud, but her mouth seemed full of cotton. How on earth was she going to face him?

Upon arriving at the hotel an hour away for their weekend honeymoon, a plan she'd not been privy to, she'd promptly holed herself up in the bathroom. What did Joey expect from her? Was this going to be a *real* marriage? She realized too late those things hadn't ever been discussed or challenged.

She could hear Joey rustling around the room, and after a half hour, he'd turned on the TV. Her new mother-in-law had packed her belongings and apparently did a little shopping. Stacey didn't own a single pair of sexy underwear or bras, but there were four new pairs of each. And she'd included some lingerie in the mix. One of them was so risqué Stacey couldn't figure out back from front or up from down.

But she did keep eyeing the pretty white satin chemise peeking from the bag. It wasn't overly sexy, but it was way less than she was accustomed to wearing.

Treading to the bag, she lifted the spaghetti strap with one finger and eyed the lingerie again. The soft knock on the door caused her to jump a foot and throw the chemise back into the bag like it was on fire. Only the fear of the man on the other side of the door kept her from laughing at herself.

"Yes?" she squeaked.

"You've been in there a while. You okay?"

Great. Now he thought she'd been *using* the bathroom or something. Way romantic. Stacey rolled her eyes at herself. What had she been thinking?

"I'm okay."

He sighed and then chuckled. "You're afraid to come out, aren't you?"

Stacey sounded so pathetic when he put it that way, but she still found herself smiling. "A little."

"I don't bite."

"I know." At least, she thought she knew. "I just need a little more time."

"Sure. I'll be out here waiting."

And that was what Stacey feared most. He was out there. *Waiting*. For *her*.

So they could...? She walked over to the satin chemise and pulled it up again, eyeing it carefully.

"Hey, Stacey?"

Stacey's hand flew to her throat. She jumped away and dropped the fabric again. This time, she jumped back into the corner of the vanity and knocked over a cup and her toothbrush.

"Stacey?" Joey's voice called, urgent now.

"I'm fine!" she shouted a little hysterically. Scrambling to put the stuff upright and making a bigger mess than she'd started with.

"This is ridiculous. Open the door." Joey wiggled the handle now.

"Don't come in, Joey!"

"What on earth is taking so long? What's that noise?"

"I just..." She was being stupid. She flung open the door in an exasperated huff and faced him.

"You just what?" he asked, worry erasing from his eyebrows and a casual grin lifting the corners of his lips.

"We haven't talk about…things."

"You mean sleeping together?"

"Yes." Stacey's cheeks burned, and it infuriated her even more she couldn't have an adult conversation without blushing like a schoolgirl. Of course, when Joey McCrary stood in front of her with an unbuttoned shirt and an undone belt, it was hard not to blush. She'd seen his six-pack before, but not since they had been married. In God's eyes, his body was hers. And oh, what a gift she'd been given.

"Well, we *are* married. But I'm not going to force you to do something you don't want to do. I was hoping you couldn't resist my charm, but since you haven't even changed out of your wedding dress, I'm thinking we might have a bust on that."

Stacey smiled. "It's not that, and you know it."

"You don't have to be scared of me, Stace."

"I'm not. This is just…awkward."

"Well, change out of your wedding dress and get comfy so we can talk or something. It won't get less awkward with you shutting yourself in here. Do you need help getting out of this contraption?" His lecherous grin told her he was trying to lighten the mood between them, but all it did was make it worse.

"No, thank you. I can manage." Then she promptly shut—and locked—the door in his face.

His chuckle didn't do much to calm her nerves.

With purpose, she strode to her bag and grabbed the chemise. She managed to wiggle out of the wedding dress and pulled the chemise over her head, not stopping to look at herself or think about her decisions.

Slinging the door open wide, she took Joey by surprise when his eyes rounded and he sat up from his casual sprawl on the bed.

"I need to stop thinking," Stacey admitted. "Otherwise, I'll think this to death, and we'll be walking on eggshells for months. Let's get this over with." There, she'd said it.

Without taking his eyes from her breasts, he clicked the TV off. He stood slowly and walked to her, each step causing her heart to trip a little more into overdrive.

"I wasn't planning on this tonight." His fingertip traced the path the spaghetti strap took over her shoulder. A shudder claimed her.

"You planned a honeymoon, a one-bed hotel room, and you didn't plan to sleep with me?" Stacey arched an eyebrow and stared at him in disbelief. He could have mentioned that sooner.

"Well, I planned to sleep in the same bed with you, yes. I thought it might be nice if we just got to know each other this weekend."

Stacey nodded. "Nice. Nice? Nice!" she shouted, smacking him in the shoulder. "You let me stay in there for an hour and a half, and you didn't think to mention maybe we'd just get to know each other instead of jumping each other's bones? *Nice*, Joey?" Yeah, hysteria ran through her veins.

And Joey had the nerve to throw his head back and laugh.

Glowering, Stacey tried to stop the angry, emotional tears stored up from the day from flowing, but they fell too fast, too hot, for her to gain control. "Is it me?" Stacey sobbed. "Did you see me in this thing your mother bought for me and decide you'd made a mistake?"

She wasn't making sense. She wished she could stop her diarrhea mouth and just go back to the bathroom for another forty-five minutes.

"No, Stace. I took one look at you, and my carefully laid plans to treat you the way you deserve to be treated went out the window. You're beautiful. I don't care if you wore a potato sack to bed, I'd still want you."

Looking into his eyes, Stacey saw he told the truth. At least, right now. He had a half-naked woman in his hotel room he just happened to be on his honeymoon with.

Cameron wouldn't have shut herself in the bathroom for over an hour to pep talk herself into having sex with her husband. They would have burst through the door, arms and legs straining, clothes flying in every direction. He would've had her on her back and screaming in less than thirty seconds.

But no, instead he was here with her. Mousy, dainty little Stacey who was still a virgin. Might stay that way if she didn't shape up and be a wife.

"Can we make a deal?" she asked.

He eyed her skeptically.

"You stop calling me beautiful, and I'll stop being such a baby."

Joey seemed to mull over the information then caustically agreed. "Okay?"

"I mean it. I don't want lies between us. We both know I'm a virgin, and this is terrifying for me. I didn't even know we were going on a honeymoon, much less going to be sleeping in the same bed. And your mom forgot to mention she'd packed *this*." She gestured toward the lingerie.

"My mama raised me to have good taste, that's for sure," he agreed.

"What are we doing, Joey? Can we just air things out right now?"

"I thought we were about to make love."

"We don't love each other," she argued.

"No," he said slowly, "but that doesn't mean we can't try. We're attracted, and we have a marriage license. Last time I checked, it meant it was okay to get naked."

With a deep breath, Stacey said, "It is. But I'm not like…her."

"Who?" She cocked an eyebrow at him, and his eyes rounded incredulously. "Cameron? You're talking about Cameron."

"Mmm."

"Stacey, I don't want you to be like her. And right now, Cameron is the furthest thing from my mind. I just want it to be you and me tonight. No talk about the future, no talk about ex-girlfriends or babies. I just want you."

She swallowed hard. Joey's eyes had fallen to her lips, and she knew the second he claimed them, she'd be lost.

Shoving at his chest, and taking a step back, she said, "I don't want either of us to regret this come morning. And we said this was going to be in name only."

"I certainly won't regret it. Will you?" He took a step forward and looped his arms around her waist. "And is a marriage in name only the way you really want this to be? Considering how attracted we are to each other? You said yourself you wanted to wait until marriage. Well? We're married. Is it really fair to either of us to prolong this torture?"

"I...I don't know." There would be no reason for regret since they were married. She'd lived up to her beliefs and hadn't had sex with a man before marriage. Now she just had to release herself from her own thoughts and let it happen.

"Tell you what. I'll get started, and if I do something you don't like, just tell me to stop. We'll take it slow, Stace. I'll do this right."

The tenderness in his eyes undid her. At least there were no pretenses, and they knew where they stood with each other. They didn't love each other, but there was no reason they couldn't enjoy the benefits of their marriage together because they cared about each other. And if Stacey was honest, this might be her only chance to get this close to a man.

"I—I just don't want to disappoint you, Joey."

A slow grin spread on his face, and his tongue darted out to lick his lips. His fingers strummed against her back and caused goosebumps to rise on her skin. "Stacey. Shut up."

Finally, a smile broke through as his lips touched hers. His hands pulled her hips against him hard, and she realized how much he truly wanted her. It felt surreal, like she wasn't really standing there in her own body but rather watching from above.

Joey's lips devoured her, his tongue plunging deep. A low groan vibrated in his chest as his fingers speared through her hair. He angled her head and took faster than she could give, but Stacey was helpless to stop him and didn't want him to. The feelings inside her were too powerful, right on the edge of something more. Just when she caught up to his fervent kiss, he pulled back.

His eyes were black with desire, and they stayed on her mouth as he spoke. "You're the most amazing kisser, Stace. I can't get enough." He claimed her lips again. Her insides melted as his hands roamed south, cupping her behind and yanking her against him.

Stacey found herself sighing when he pulled away again.

"Are you okay? I know I should go slower, and I will. But right now, I just need to feel you."

Feeling was exactly what she wanted. "Joey. Shut up."

With a chuckle, he lifted her until she wrapped her legs around his waist. "Promise you'll wear this for me again."

At the moment, Stacey would promise anything. "Mmm."

"Promise me, Stace. I want all of you, not just the part helping me get my baby."

"I thought we said no talking about the

future or babies."

"I'm talking about you, Stace. I want us to have a real marriage. None of this name-only stuff. I want to be the husband you deserve and be all the things you've ever dreamed of having."

Going still in his arms, Stacey then averted her gaze and then dropped her legs. "Put me down, Joey."

He did as she asked and frowned down at her. His hands crossed against the expanse of his chest.

They stared at one another for a long while as Stacey gathered her bearings. She wasn't sure where to begin, so she let her heart do the talking.

"I can't promise you anything, Joey. You're the one who made it clear this wasn't a love match. And I'm okay. I've got both eyes open. But I can't have you confusing me with all the pretty words and promises to be a good husband. We didn't get married to have a honeymoon or to make love. We got married to get your baby back. Anything else, we'll just have to take it a day at a time."

"Stace—"

She held up her hand, effectively silencing him. "I'm not pretty. I'm not sexy. I'm nothing like the other women you've been with. I don't hold any illusions; you feel guilty over this, and you want to make it up to me. It shows your character that you want to be a good husband. In truth, we can't go back and undo it. In God's eyes, we're married, and we should stay this way until one of us cheats or dies. I do want to make the best of this. I really do, but…" She licked her lips and settled her stare on Joey's worried frown. "…I'm not ready to sleep with you. I know I'm your wife, and I'm more than willing, but to you, it's just a means to an end. I'm not saying it's wrong to feel attracted. We're married now. But I don't want to be just a warm body for you. I guess I'm holding out hope maybe one day you can look past the glasses and my miserable wardrobe and see me for who I am. When you've done that, I'll be satisfied with wherever it takes us."

"You seem to know an awful lot," Joey grumbled.

"I'm just being real."

"You're being ridiculous."

"Maybe to you."

"I'm pretty sure if anyone else were here, they'd think you were being ridiculous, too."

"Let's just get some sleep. I'm exhausted." Stacey turned around and crawled into bed, pulling the covers up to her ears. Joey hadn't moved.

"I can't sleep next to you while you're wearing *that*."

"There's a couch right over there." Anger simmered near the surface now, just waiting to erupt. Usually, Stacey wasn't easy to anger, but everything was starting to take its toll on what little confidence she had.

"There is no way I'm sleeping on the couch on my honeymoon."

"Then don't." Stacey snuggled a little deeper into the sheets and closed her eyes.

Before she fully registered what happened, the covers were gone and she was underneath Joey, his eyes blazing with an odd mixture of playfulness and determination.

He settled between her legs, and his lips trailed a heated path down her neck and over her collarbone. She hated the wanton whimper escaping her mouth, so she clamped her eyes and mouth shut.

"I'm going to break down your defenses one by one, Stace. One by one. Before long, you'll be demanding I make love to you just like this."

He continued to demonstrate his power over her body by touching and trailing searing paths of heat along her skin to the most intimate places. She wasn't afraid of his body or the pain inevitably involved. What she was afraid of was the repercussions of such an intimate act with him. Her heart was at stake. Papa had taken most of it when he'd passed on. Joey was getting the remnants, and she wanted to hold on to those and not feel so exposed. But as it was, she knew it was a losing battle.

"Stacey?" he asked, looking up into her face. His eyes were rounded and vulnerable. "I want to make love to you. Tonight. Will you let me?"

Stacey swallowed thickly. Her body betrayed her, arching up to him involuntarily. She might be just a warm body to him. He might even close his eyes and envision Cameron as he made love to her.

But she could pretend, too. Tonight, he loved her for who she was, thought she was sexy and beautiful, and their marriage was a real one.

Tomorrow, she'd deal with the consequences.

Pressing her lips to his, she wrapped her arms and legs around him, telling him the answer without a single word.

CHAPTER SEVEN

A PINPRICK of light annoyed Joey from behind his eyelids. Exhaustion wasn't done wreaking havoc with his body, and it didn't help he'd had a late night last night.

With a jolt, Joey opened his eyes and saw a sleeping Stacey lying next to him. He wasn't one to pride himself on things, but this morning she looked thoroughly loved. From her tousled hair down to her wrinkled gown. Cleavage peeked at him from behind her arm. He couldn't resist running a finger down the line and pressing his lips to her forehead.

Stacey Ingram surprised him. They'd gone back and forth for so long last night he feared the night was lost to them. But if he was anything, he was determined and even if he didn't love her, he wanted to be a good husband and show her what the physical side of a relationship felt like. And if he was honest, it was no hardship for him. Stacey was as passionate between the sheets as she was about everything else in her life.

And he was counting on passion to get them through the next few years together as they raised the baby.

At some point during the night, she'd taken her contacts out and placed her glasses on the nightstand beside her. The duct tape stared back at him like some sort of joke. The first thing they were doing was getting those fixed or replaced when they got home. Maybe she'd consider wearing contacts more often. He hated for those beautiful eyes of hers to be hidden. He'd found out last night how expressive they could be when her defenses were down.

Stacey stirred and flipped on her back, the gown shifting and rising on her thigh. He placed his palm there and traced circles with his thumb. Then he delivered a single kiss next to his hand.

Glancing up, he saw she stared at the ceiling, wide-eyed and alert. Sliding his hands up the side of her waist, his body followed and pinned her to the bed.

"Good morning, Ms. McCrary," he whispered, kissing the underside of her jaw.

"Morning," she snapped and pushed at him.

"Uh-uh," he argued. "We're not going to be all weird today. This is the first day of our honeymoon, and it's going to count."

"Joey…"

"Shut up and kiss me, Wife."

It didn't take her long before she grinned and gave him a chaste peck on the lips.

"Nope, a good one."

She turned her head to the side and shook her head. "Morning breath."

"Morning breath? Really, that's your excuse?"

She stared at him and then grinned. "Has anyone ever told you you're relentless? I'm sore in places I didn't know I had."

"You know what that means, right?" he asked, then kissed her long and deep.

When he pulled away she shook her head. "What?"

"It means we just have to get you broken in a little more. Like leather. The more you use it, the better it gets."

A saccharine sweet smile lit her features. "How romantic!"

Throwing his head back, he laughed heartily. "C'mon, Stace. You know you want to."

Chewing on her bottom lip, a little habit he'd noticed her doing when she was thinking, she finally nodded. "I do want you."

Desire shot through his veins. The sweetest words ever uttered. "Then sit back, my lady, and enjoy the ride. Before we leave this hotel room, you're going to know what an orgasm feels like."

With a roll of her eyes, Stacey met him halfway for a kiss. The confidence of her touch spurred him on. The previous night hadn't been ideal, but then again, Stacey had been a virgin, and he'd forgotten to read up on how to speed the process along for someone terrified out of her mind. But it wasn't anything a little experience and a little more patience wouldn't cure.

Waggling his eyebrows, he trailed a path of hot kisses down her torso until he reached his goal. Before long, he was lost in Stacey's passion.

SWEAT BEADED on Stacey's forehead. Who on earth had she married? Joey was insatiable, and it seemed he was in no rush for food, water, or clothing, all of which Stacey would give her right arm for at that moment.

As Joey collapsed on top of her, spent, she ran her fingernails down his back. He shuddered.

"You're so perfect," he rasped. "I can't get enough."

"You're telling me this?" she countered. At his chuckle, she smiled and pushed at his shoulders. "C'mon, Joey. It's afternoon. I need food if I'm going to survive this."

"Good plan. Shower together?" he asked as he raised a brow, turning on the charm.

"For no other purpose than to get clean or do you have ulterior motives?"

"I'm not sure. I guess we'll find out when we get there?"

With a quick peck on the lips, Joey helped her up. She then realized she'd removed her contacts. She blindly patted the nightstand for her glasses.

"Here you go." Joey placed her glasses on her nose with careful precision. "Better?"

Suddenly self-conscious, Stacey looked down. Her world might be a little *too* focused now. With Joey standing before her in his birthday suit, and her in a skimpy chemise, the reality of their new life settled around her like a mound of falling debris.

"Why don't you wear contacts more often?" Joey casually asked.

Stacey shrugged. "Too expensive."

"Would you like to wear them more often? I can tell you're not confident when you have your glasses on. I have a good job now, and we can afford to keep you in contacts. But it's your call. At the very least, let's get your glasses fixed." Joey's hand enclosed around hers, and he smiled.

"If you want..." Stacey replied.

"I do. You just think about it, and let me know what you want to do."

"I will."

Suddenly, her world tilted, and it took her a moment to realize Joey had scooped her off her feet and walked into the bathroom with her. Planting a sweet kiss on the tip of her nose, he put her on her feet again and reached behind her to turn the shower on. Then he took a step back, just enough for him to grab the hem of her nighty and pull it over her head.

Even though they'd made love several times during the night, Stacey hadn't undressed completely. Instead, Joey had seemed content to kiss her through the fabric and leave the small barrier between them. Now, she bared it all before him, and his eyes were rounded with desire yet again.

"Seriously, Joey, I need food."

"I need *you*," he murmured.

With a deep sigh, not born completely from frustration but rather excitement, she let Joey usher her into the shower.

She wasn't sure how a honeymoon was supposed to play out, but this was shaping up to be a pretty good one.

SEVERAL HOURS later, Joey inhaled a hotdog with chili as he sat next to Stacey on a park bench downtown. She carefully ate her pretzel as he licked the chili away from his chin. He gave her a smile and winked.

"Hungry?" she asked with a chuckle.

"Just in a hurry to get back to the hotel room."

She gave a little smile and shook her head, even as pink tinged her cheeks. "When is Cameron due?"

"A few more weeks. When we get back, we need to start thinking about a nursery and names."

Stacey frowned and shook her head. "Names are between you and Cameron."

Wadding up his hotdog paper and napkin, he tossed them in the trash next to Stacey. "Cameron has no rights to her baby right now. She's signed everything over to me already until she's out of prison, Stace."

"Doesn't mean I should be involved in the process of naming the baby."

Joey engulfed her hand with his large one. "You're my wife. This baby is going to call you Mama. You have every right to name her."

"It's a girl?"

"Last check with the ultrasound tech, it was."

Stacey leaned back against the bench, clearly perplexed. It was almost as if Joey could hear her thoughts. During those younger years, she didn't do frilly or play with dolls or know how to fix hair. All she said she remembered when she was a kid was playing in the dirt and coming home to a scolding. Climbing trees was more her thing.

"I know what you're thinking."

"What, Einstein?" She studied the simple gold band on his ring finger she'd placed there yesterday. He loved the way it looked on him, even if it was a little surreal. Stacey, the girl he'd worshiped, still worshiped if the truth be told, was his wife. He sent up a prayer of thanks. Joey wasn't sure what God had in store for him or if the devil was wielding his power over his life, but either way, he was enjoying being her husband so far.

"You're thinking you don't do pink. You have no idea how to do girlie stuff, right?"

A smile slipped passed her obvious worry. "Exactly."

Joey chuckled and pulled her close, placing

a kiss in her hair. "Let me tell you, Stacey McCrary. You're going to be the best mom to our little girl, and she's going to love you no matter what. Even if she finds out your favorite color is green and not pink."

"How did you remember?" she asked, looking into his eyes.

"I still remember the day you put a gross frog on my leg!"

"And you screamed like a girl." Her giggling made him smile.

"More like a boy who had to face his fears without any prep time!"

Stacey laughed. "Big ole baby," she chided.

"I used to get so angry that you weren't scared of anything."

"I was scared of a lot. I still am."

"I'm scared of you, Stace. You've always scared me." He sobered, thinking of the lightness in his heart and the way he looked forward to getting home and settling into a routine with her. Waking up next to her every morning. Six months ago, settling down was the last thing on his to-do list.

"No reason for me to scare you. I'm just a girl you grew up with."

"Who's now my wife and knows how terrified I am of frogs."

"Be nice to me, and you have nothing to worry about." She grinned, and he felt a tug of tenderness he hadn't experienced since Cameron. He shoved it quickly away and cleared his throat.

"I'll be nice all right," he drawled, eyeing her with playfulness. "My mama always taught me if I couldn't be nice, I wouldn't get rewarded."

Stacey's eyebrows rose.

"All I know is I must have been nice somewhere along the way. I sure got rewarded this time."

Shoving her glasses up on her nose, she sniffed and looked off into the distance, clearly lost in thought. He'd never understand her.

"What did I say wrong?"

"I thought we said no more flattery, no more sugar coating. I'm not a reward. I made a decision to help you." She shrugged and looked away again. "Just because we've had sex now doesn't mean you have to say flowery things. I'm well aware of who and what I am to you."

Reluctant to get *that* conversation started again, he squeezed her hand at the end of a sigh. He didn't want to dwell on the fact she had called what they did last night *sex*. They may not love each other, but it was a far cry from just sex. "Have you ever thought about baby names?"

"I told you it's not my call. You name her what you want to name her."

He growled this time, taking her by the shoulders and turning her to look directly into her surprised eyes. "What's it gonna take? You've already married me, Stace. She's yours, too. We're going to be raising her. I want your input."

Stacey closed her eyes and pressed her lips together. Then she said, "I've always loved the name Rachel."

Joey mulled it over in his mind, but before he could speak, she stood. "But again, it's not my call. She's your kid."

Joey grinned at her self-consciousness and grabbed her wrist as she paced past him. He hauled her in his lap and brushed her runaway hair behind her ear. "I think Rachel is a beautiful name. I like it."

Disbelief clouded her eyes. "Really?"

"Rachel from the Bible. Jacob loved her and worked so hard for her."

"Just like you will," Stacey said with a smile.

"Are you ready to be a mother?"

"It's all I've thought about since we've agreed to do this. I've always wanted to be a mom."

"At least I did something right, huh?"

A careless shrug lifted Stacey's shoulders, and she looked away again. "We'll see. My mom was great, but as time fades, I'm forgetting things. I might not be a natural at parenting."

"Hence why there are two of us. We'll do it together."

They sat like that, Stacey on his lap and Joey rubbing her back in silence for a while. He'd give his right arm to know what she was thinking about, but then again, he might regret finding out. What if she regretted him? What if she didn't bond with the baby? He'd heard of it happening in adoption.

"Joey?"

"Yeah?"

A gust of wind lifted her blonde curls and they teased his nose. "Cameron has a few days after she's born to change her mind, doesn't she?"

Joey's eyes slammed shut and he swallowed thickly. "I doubt she will."

"But the possibility is still there?"

"Yes."

"So if she changes her mind, where does that leave me?"

"Still my wife. Still the only stable mother my baby girl is gonna have."

"You don't think it's possible for her to change once she sees her?"

Stacey had suddenly voiced his fears without him realizing what he'd been afraid of all along. What if Cameron straightened out and wanted him back? Where would it leave Stacey?

Looking at her now, he knew he'd be hard pressed to choose. He'd cared about Cameron with a reckless passion he'd always remember. Few people found their kind of passion. But he enjoyed Stacey in a quiet, no strings attached friendship that held equal amounts of sway. Both were powerful, but he stood less of a chance of getting hurt with Stacey.

He'd promised her no divorce. But when he thought about Cameron coming back to him, clean and ready to raise their family, he wasn't sure how he'd feel.

"I think it's possible," he said carefully. "But she's pretty bad off. Regardless of what she decides, we will still have her until Cameron gets out of jail."

Stacey shifted in his lap and placed her hand on his shoulder. "I know you love her. If it comes down to it, I couldn't ask you to stay with me when I know you wish things were different with her."

A lump rose in his throat, swift and choking. She was still the same self-sacrificing girl she'd been when she'd turned eight and had given him her last birthday cookie even though he'd had three already. He touched her jaw and smoothed his thumb over her skin. "I married you, Stacey. No, it wasn't for love, but I would never abandon you. If Cameron changes her mind about the baby, we'll deal with it then. I don't know how I'd feel. For now, let's stop all this heavy talk and experience our honeymoon. We've barely been married twenty-four hours, and I want to enjoy this weekend, not dwell on what-ifs."

Stacey's lips turned up hesitantly. "Me, too."

"Wanna go back to the hotel room now?" He wiggled his eyebrows and winked.

Stacey threw her head back and laughed, an action that left him breathless and in awe of her beauty. She didn't care if she laughed a little too loud or if her butt bone was digging into his thigh. She simply flung her arms around his neck and hugged him close, something Joey was glad to reciprocate.

CHAPTER EIGHT

THE WEEKEND passed in a blur of sightseeing, hiking, and sex. If nothing else, Stacey had come to realize one very important thing during their time together thus far: Joey was a patient lover. Despite her inability to have an orgasm, everything Joey did felt amazing. But she suspected her lack of completion had more to do with their distant emotional connection. Not once had he said anything that rang true.

Sure, he'd poured it on thick with his fancy words and his fancy bedroom techniques, but when it all boiled down, all that was left between them was simply a shared childhood and a common goal: To provide a mother and father for his baby girl. But what happened when the baby realized her parents were a sham?

The more Stacey thought about it, the more she started to regret her rash decision. Overcompensating for her own loss when the baby would eventually know the real reasons behind their marriage made her worry the baby would grow to regret her and resent them together. And what if Cameron did straighten her life out and decide she wanted a go at her and Joey's relationship again? Stacey had no doubts Joey would divorce her as quickly as he'd married her. What was it her mother had always said? Once a player always a player? Player was a good description for Joey's college days, and he'd been out of college all of eight weeks.

Stacey prayed for their marriage, for Cameron's health and determination, for the baby's health, and for Joey's peace of mind, whatever that meant in the long run. If Cameron made him happy, then he should be with Cameron.

But of course that brought to mind where it would leave her. She'd be emotionally attached to a child who wasn't hers, married to a man who didn't love her, and left in the same position she'd been in before they'd married.

Alone.

If there was one thing Stacey hated, it was being alone.

The following Monday came after their honeymoon, and waking up with Joey in her bed felt odd in her childhood home, almost like she was doing something wrong. What if Papa could see them from where he was? A blush heated her cheeks, and she was thankful Joey hadn't hinted at getting naked last night. Instead, they'd shared a quiet dinner with his parents at their house, and he'd gone to bed, rolling over and snoring softly within a few minutes. She knew she shouldn't feel cheated, and it would have felt awkward, but at the very least, he could have told her goodnight. But the honeymoon was over, literally and figuratively, and it was time to get down to business. Cameron was due to give birth in only a couple of weeks.

Stacey rose while Joey was in the shower and cooked him a simple breakfast of eggs and toast. She remembered from the younger years he liked scrambled eggs with a touch of mustard in them – weird, but hopefully still to his liking. She buttered the toast and put grape jelly on it. After pouring him some orange juice, she stood back and looked at the first meal she'd prepared for her husband.

Her shoulders sagged. It was pathetic. They'd been gone for a few days so she hadn't had a chance to get groceries like she usually did on Sunday after church. She'd have to make sure she went today so she could make a nice dinner for him to come home to.

Joey exited the bathroom with a towel hung low on his hips and using another towel to dry his hair. Little lines of water still clung to his chest, and she tried not to stare, but really. His body was one of a god, and for the time being, he was all hers.

Looking away quickly, she shoved her glasses up on her nose and sniffed. She didn't want to test the theory of how awkward it would feel to have sex in her childhood bed. Not yet. She'd have to mentally prepare for it.

"Wow, you cooked breakfast." He eyed the plate and then her as he walked barefoot over to her and gave her a chaste kiss on the lips. "Thank you. I usually just grab an apple or banana."

Lurching toward the table, she stuttered, "I'm…s…sorry, Joey. I didn't know. I can eat it or just throw it away. I thought—"

Joey's warm fingers surrounded her wrists and tugged her close. "Stacey. It's great. Thank you."

"Do you still like mustard in your eggs?" she asked weakly, hating how she felt in his presence.

"I love it."

Something in his eyes gave her pause. He seemed to glow, his smile sweet instead of predatory. His eyes took her in, and a small grin graced the corners of his lips. "You're amazing."

Stacey snorted a laugh. "Just eat."

Pulling away from his embrace, she moved to the living room and grabbed her Bible. It had been a few days since she'd read anything, and she needed to freshen up on her husband and wife verses. Considering she'd never really felt like those would apply to her, she had to read up on her responsibilities to her new husband.

Husband.

The thought still brought a shiver to her spine. A good one.

A little while later, Joey walked into the living room, his hair still wet from his shower and his amazing cologne preceding him. He tightened his tie and shrugged on his coat. Once he settled, he came over and sat next to her.

"So, this weekend, I'm going to need to visit Cameron at the prison."

Stacey found she couldn't move. She couldn't breathe or even process the statement. Why? Wouldn't the state notify him when it was time to get his kid? Why did he need to see her?

As if reading her mind, he said, "I know it's not the best timing, but I'd like to tell her I'm married now and make sure she knows you're going to be raising Rachel."

"Rachel?" she squeaked.

"I thought we agreed on what we were going to name her." Joey's eyes searched hers, but there were no emotions Stacey could place.

"We never agreed on anything."

"I like that name, Stacey. I haven't seen her yet, but unless we both agree Rachel doesn't fit her, I think it'll be perfect."

Stacey could feel a boundary around her heart settling in the cold corners. She didn't want him to do this to her. He was going to see the woman he freely admitted to loving when he didn't even have to.

"You can do whatever you'd like, Joey. I'm sure Cameron would like to know, too."

"Will you go with me?" he asked, taking her hand and kissing her fingertips.

She looked at him and frowned. "I don't think so, Joey. It's asking too much."

"Why?"

"Because!" She stood and retreated to the corner of the room, a habit of hers when Joey made her uncomfortable. "I'm, like, the *other* woman. She'll hate me once she realizes my role and how actively I planned to take her child. I'd hate me, too."

Joey stood and slowly sauntered toward her. "It's impossible to hate you, Stacey. I've spent my entire life knowing you and being your friend. I know Cameron well enough to know she might even be appreciative for what you've given up to help me take care of Rachel."

Stacey's heart pounded. She didn't want to hear this. It was just flowery words meant to woo her and make her see things his way, but the fact was, he'd used her and she'd let him. She was okay with it for now, but she wouldn't be a pushover.

"I won't go with you, Joey," she said as she squared her shoulders and lifted her chin. This was something she felt pretty strongly about and he wouldn't change her mind.

"I need you, Stacey. I don't think I can go by myself."

Well, then. The answer was simple. "Then don't go."

"I need to make sure she knows we're over."

Stacey closed her eyes and shook her head at his callousness. "And what better way than to bring your new wife with you to rub it in her face."

"Stacey—"

"I'm not going with you. End of the discussion." She slipped away from him and carefully locked herself inside the bathroom. A few moments later, she watched from the small window as he got in his car and drove away.

Reality was settling hard on top of her. What had she done?

JOEY FELT like crying. He wouldn't, of course, but if it had been any other place and any other time of day, he might have just decided to let go and let the tears fall. Stacey was killing him bit by bit. He was beginning to live for those rare smiles and even rarer displays of affection. It seemed the only place he could get those from her was in bed, and since coming home, things had shifted for him. Was it fair to have a sexual relationship with her when they both knew it wasn't for love?

He didn't hear her complaining, but she'd also gone to bed a half hour before him last night. She wasn't asleep when he came to bed, but she made no movement, like a stone statue, and he assumed she was off limits. He would give her time to get used to him being a part of her familiar surroundings. A novice he wasn't when it came to women, and he figured he'd know when she was ready to get back to the physical aspect of marriage.

Of course, the thought had crossed his mind that maybe she didn't like the physical side. There had certainly been no movement forward since their wedding night in the enjoyment department, but he wasn't a sore loser and he was determined. She'd given up so much for him he was pretty sure he at least owed her some good sex. They were married after all.

He drove to work silently, thinking of Stacey, trying to fight the constant nagging that he was missing something with her. But what?

His cell phone rang just as he pulled into the parking lot. He didn't recognize the number.

"This is Joseph McCrary," he said as he gathered his things for work.

"Mr. McCrary, this is Warden Mitchell at the Prison. We have on record you'd like to be notified when prisoner Cameron Matheson goes into labor. She's being transported to University Hospital as we speak. At last check, her water had broken and she was about five centimeters dilated."

Joey's heart constricted. He was about to become a father. Rachel would be here soon.

And once he told his boss what was going on, he'd be seeing Cameron for the first time since she told him he was going to be a daddy.

The thought scared him to death.

STACEY SAT in the waiting room, fidgeting and pushing her glasses up on her nose in a nervous habit. Joey had been in the hospital room with Cameron ever since they'd arrived almost two hours ago. As usual, she sat alone, waiting for a crumb of information on whether or not her childhood best friend was a father.

Envisioning Joey as a father made her want to giggle. She knew he'd be amazing, but she could still remember him in the "all girls have cooties" phase. Funny how she'd been the only girl he'd still talked to during that time. Of course, by high school, he'd definitely grown out of it and moved on to greener pastures. Pastures where girls like her didn't graze.

But it was okay. Stacey had long accepted she was what many would call a nerd or a Jesus freak. She just wished she could be a little more for Joey because all of his friends would expect that when or if she ever met them. She tried not to feel sorry for herself, but it was next to impossible knowing her husband was with the love of his life, watching their child be born.

Suddenly the double doors in front of her swung open and Joey came rushing out, clad in scrubs and a facemask. "C'mon, Stacey! Cameron agreed for you to be in there, too! She's about to deliver!"

On instinct, and mainly for Joey, she rushed to him. He took her by the arm and practically dragged her down the sterile halls. As they slowed to a door with a prison guard outside, Stacey tried to take it all in.

It was too quiet. She wasn't sure what she'd expected, but calm wasn't it. She could sense Joey's excitement, but as she walked in, she never expected to see the mother-to-be, reclined with legs up, looking at her with sparkling blue eyes.

"You must be Stacey," she said, extending a graceful hand as far as the handcuff would allow. Stacey awkwardly took it and squeezed gently. She had no idea what to say and couldn't think past the woman's beauty. Blonde hair she figured had once been long and beautiful flowed down to her shoulders but ended in a blunt and somewhat uneven cut. Those blue eyes sparkled with tears and her pink lips gave Stacey a brave smile.

"I hear you've done a great thing for Joe, here."

Stacey simply stared. *Joe?*

"If you're going to raise my baby, I want you to be here, too."

Stacey looked to Joey for help. She didn't want to say anything to upset her, nor did she want her to think she wouldn't be a good mother to Rachel.

Joey stepped in front of her and took Cameron's hand. The look on his face told of his undying love and devotion for the beautiful woman. Stacey felt like an intruder on their special moment.

"I don't think I should be in here," Stacey murmured to Joey.

He turned distracted eyes on her and shook his head. "You need to stay."

The hustle around her increased, and she found a safe corner out of everyone's way. A nurse prepped what appeared to be a baby bed with a heat light, and the bed Cameron labored on was broken down.

"Don't push just yet, Ms. Matheson."

But even as he said the words, Cameron pushed, graceful even in pain, and the doctor rushed to finish putting on his gloves. "I think we're going to have a baby in a few more pushes!" he encouraged. They waited for the next contraction, and she pushed again.

All the while, Joey's eyes never left Cameron's face. He gently pushed her hair back from her sweaty face and mumbled, "Baby, you're doing a great job. You can do this. She's going to be so beautiful."

Stacey allowed herself one selfish tear and then sat up straight, watching the miracle of birth. Would she ever be lying on a bed giving birth to a baby with a man who loved her so deeply? Would she ever experience the changes her body was made for?

After two more pushes, Rachel made a screaming debut into the world, none too happy about her cold new environment. She was immediately placed on Cameron's belly, and Joey cut the umbilical cord, just like any other happy father. The nurses and doctor rubbed her down to stimulate blood flow and cleaned her off, and then she was whisked away to the warmer where she was measured and footprinted.

Cameron and Joey never took their eyes off Rachel, and occasionally Joey would place a tender kiss on Cameron's temple. At one point, she smiled tiredly at him and placed her palm on his cheek. Stacey *was* the intruder. She wasn't really sure why Joey had insisted on her being present, but now she knew it was a mistake.

Silently and unnoticed, she slipped outside and leaned against the wall outside. They needed their time alone to rejoice in their creation and not to feel guilty over their feelings. Cameron had made some bad decisions, but it didn't mean she was a bad person. If Joey loved her as much as it appeared he did, she couldn't be all bad and Stacey couldn't hold his love for the other woman against him. She'd gone into this with both of her eyes open, and she refused to be hurt over it.

The last few days had gone by like a spinning top, and she wasn't even used to the ring on her finger, let alone the fact she played second fiddle to a beautiful prisoner. It was a place she'd learn to accept so she could experience motherhood, even if only until Cameron got out and came back for Joey and

Rachel.

The lone tear she'd shed in the delivery room wasn't enough. She needed to let out her feelings or it would destroy her. Running to the nearest bathroom, she locked the door and let out her sobs, allowing her feelings to run their course so she could be stronger for Joey when the time came...and stronger for herself.

Yes, she'd always been the one who wasn't quite accepted, and her whole life she'd been okay with the stigma. Why did it have to change now? Why did a woman in handcuffs have to bring her to her knees, quite literally, for her to finally realize she'd made a huge mistake when she married Joey?

CHAPTER NINE

JOEY PLAYED the doting father quite well, because when he looked at Rachel, a perfect mix of him and Cameron, he could see only love. She weighed in at a perfect 8 pounds and 7 ounces, was 21 inches long and had baby blues and blonde hair just like her mother. Joey cried tears of joy she was here safely and Cameron was okay.

After she was checked out and found to be healthy, the nurses swaddled her small body and handed her over. The moment she was placed in his arms, his heart did funny things. He was so madly in love with one tiny, eight-pound baby, he knew he'd never be the same again.

One person's face came to mind when he turned. He had to share this moment with Stacey. There was no one who could understand him the way Stacey did, and no one else could understand the impact this moment had had on their lives.

"Stacey, come look at her, she's so beautiful!" He looked up but Stacey wasn't where she'd been when Cameron was about to deliver. She was nowhere to be seen. "Stacey?"

"Are you talking about the blonde in the corner?" the doctor asked.

"Yeah."

"She left about five minutes ago, right after the baby was born. Looked like she was in a hurry."

Odd. He thought she'd want to be here to hold Rachel and get to know her. If the moment hadn't been so amazing, he might have been a little miffed she deserted him, but he tried not to dwell on it. Instead, he looked down at his daughter and put his finger in her tiny palm. She immediately grabbed it and smacked her mouth, turning her head to the side. He'd deal with how he'd upset his wife later. Right now, all that mattered was Rachel.

"What does this mean?" he asked the nurse standing nearby.

"She's rooting. She's hungry. Would you

like to feed her, Mama?"

He looked up to Cameron's surprised face. He wasn't sure it was a good idea for her to get too attached. But then again, what better way to encourage her to be a better person than to see the life depending on her?

In the end, he couldn't deny her. It was her baby, too. Just because she signed legal rights away until she got out of prison didn't mean she didn't deserve to have some good memories. And if she proved she could stay clean, Joey couldn't keep her from being a part of Rachel's life later on. Rachel would need to know her mother hadn't abandoned her.

Cameron sat up as best she could now that she was stitched and the epidural was wearing off. She tugged at one shoulder of her gown, pulling it down and exposing her breast. Joey placed Rachel in her arms and let her work her motherly magic. Before long, Rachel latched on and sucked like a champ.

With tear-filled eyes, Cameron looked up at him. "I wish I hadn't made so many stupid decisions," she said. "This could be a normal us, and that could be the ring I put on your finger."

Joey swallowed thickly. He had once dreamed of her saying those words, but now a different reality belonged to him. "You didn't want to get married, remember?"

"I did, Joe. I just didn't know how to tell

you all my secrets."

"So you got arrested so I'd find out the hard way?"

"No. Like I said. A lot of stupid choices. I'd give anything to be the kind of mother Rachel deserves."

"Me, too." Joey looked away and paced a little before turning back to her. "Stacey's a good woman. I've known her since we were kids. She'll treat Rachel like she was her own."

"Do you love her?" Cameron asked absently, stroking Rachel's cheek.

"I couldn't imagine my life without her. We've been best friends since we were kids."

Cameron shook her head, and he was once again shocked by the changes in her appearance. Her shorn hair, small frame, even her teeth looked a little yellow.

"I still love you, Joe. I know it's not much coming from a prisoner, but I don't think I'll ever stop loving you. Just always know that, okay? I want you to be happy, no matter what."

Joey shifted in his seat, suddenly uncomfortable with the turn in conversation. Instead, he focused on his daughter and pushed the conversation back to her. "Thank you for her. And for making the right decisions about her welfare. You know I'll love her and give her everything possible."

"I do know. I didn't get to talk to Stacey,

but she seems sweet. Just don't make her think she's living in my shadow. She's probably pretty unsure of herself right now and where she belongs in all this."

Joey sighed. "Yeah. Confidence isn't her specialty."

"It should be," Cameron said softly. "She snagged the best guy in the world."

With a chuckle, he shoved his hands in his pockets. "I better go find her and make sure she's okay."

Cameron raised her shackled hand and gave him a wry grin. "Go on. I'm not going anywhere."

He rolled his eyes playfully and walked out of the room. Just outside the door, Stacey was sitting against the wall, knees to her chest. It was clear she'd been crying. What a mess this all was.

"Your parents are in the waiting room. I think Cameron's are, too. I didn't feel like going out there explaining who I was to Cameron's family."

Without a word, he sat down next to her with a grunt and took her hand in his. It shouldn't have surprised him, but she carefully extracted it only moments later. "Congratulations on becoming a father."

"Thanks," he mumbled, unsure of what to say next. After a moment, he finally asked the question burning in his mind. "Why did you leave?"

Stacey's eyes were closed, but she licked her lips. A telltale sign she was buying time before answering. "Let's just say it was all a bit emotional."

"Are you okay?"

"I'm fine." But the words were said too quickly and too chipper for him to really believe her.

"She's beautiful, isn't she?"

"She's going to be an amazing little girl," Stacey said with conviction.

"Only because you're going to raise her. You're pretty amazing, too, Stace."

Joey didn't have time to finish her name before she was standing. "I think I'll go get Cameron some flowers. Do you need anything?"

Confusion swept over him at her change in attitude, but he went along because he could only stand so much drama in one day. "I could use some water. Thanks, baby."

He stood only to be nose-to-nose with an angry Stacey, her finger poking into his chest. "Don't ever call me your baby again." Her eyes burned bright, and her mouth was drawn into a tight frown.

Holding out his hands, he frowned. "Okay. I'll try to remember."

"Don't try. Remember."

Rachel's cry distracted him enough not to respond as she turned and stalked away, but he filed it away in his mind to ask her about later.

A KNOCK ON the door the next morning had Stacey out of bed and alert before she even exited her bedroom. Was it Joey? He hadn't come home last night, and she assumed he'd stayed with Cameron at the hospital. No phone call, no text telling her not to wait up.

With a deep breath, Stacey opened the door and exhaled when she saw it was Joey's mom.

"Ms. McCrary! I thought you'd be at the hospital by now, seeing that beautiful new granddaughter of yours."

"I'm headed there in a bit," she said as she stepped in, uninvited. "We need to talk, honey."

A deep sigh escaped as her heart began to pound. "What about?"

"You know what about. This whole situation is so convoluted, Stacey. I know you must be drowning."

The understatement of the century. "I'm fine."

"You're not fine. I saw you crying in the hallway yesterday. I know you've always loved him. He's hard not to love."

Stacey bit her lip. "I do love him, but I keep praying it'll fade so it won't hurt so much."

"Give him time. I think you guys are perfect for each other, but this marriage was awfully quick. You haven't even been married a week and now you're parents. It's a lot to take in."

The lump in Stacey's throat kept her from saying anything.

"Is he good to you?" Ms. McCrary's hand settled on top of hers. Something her own mother might have done. What she wouldn't give to have her mom there for some good advice.

"He's wonderful. More than I could have ever asked for."

"But…?"

Stacey smiled. "Nothing."

"I've known you since you were born. I was a best friend to your mother until the day she died. I know when something's bothering you."

Should she let it out? Could she? This was her husband's mother she was talking to. Even if she spoke her fears aloud, would they be safe with her? Regardless, Stacey needed someone to talk to. If it got back to Joey, it would be less she'd have to explain to him later.

"How do I compete with her? We never agreed this was love, and I'm happy to help him. I know what it's like not to have your parents together, and I'm so happy Joey wanted his little girl to have a mother and a father. But kids are smart. Rachel will pick up on the fact we don't have a real marriage. What then?"

"Honestly? I don't think you have anything to worry about."

"What if she comes back and wants Rachel and Joey? After what I saw yesterday between them, I don't think I'd be wrong to say he'd choose her."

"Things are still raw, Stace. He loved Cameron, but I think he grew to love the idea of her. She's beautiful, yes, but not many people can say they married their best friend. Love or not, you two know each other much better than he and Cameron did. She's a sweet girl, but I think until she gets her addiction under control and can support herself and a kid, the state would never grant her rights."

Stacey sat in silence. She didn't know how to tell Ms. McCrary those things were the least of her concerns.

"But that's not what you're talking about, is it?"

"You're a mind reader." Stacey grinned.

"He loves you, honey. Maybe not the way you want him to right now, but if you give him time, he'll see what's right in front of him."

"It's been twenty years. If he doesn't see it

by now, I don't think he will."

"You never know what prayer can do. And the fact you came into this with no expectations is half the battle."

"I just want to be beautiful for him."

Ms. McCrary studied Stacey, her perfectly coifed hair and neatly pressed suit screamed beauty and maintenance. Even her toenails were free of chipped polish, unlike her own. "Until you're beautiful to yourself, you'll never be beautiful for him."

It sounded like something her mother would have said. It was these rare moments that hit her like a lead weight falling from the heavens. Her mother might not be with her in the physical sense, but she was still helping her and guiding her from heaven. She had to be.

"Agreed." Stacey gave her a smile and moved her hand away. "It's time I get ready to go to the hospital myself. I'm sure Joey would like a change of clothes and a toothbrush."

"He didn't come home last night?" Ms. McCrary's body language suddenly changed, and she sat up straighter.

"No. I figured he stayed at the hospital with Cameron."

She sighed and shook her head, a frown marring her pretty features. "I guess we'll see. If you're right, I might just have to string him up by his toes."

CHAPTER TEN

WHEN STACEY entered the hospital, she wasn't sure what awaited her. For some reason, she envisioned Joey spooning Cameron in her hospital bed while Rachel slept soundly in her bassinet next to them.

Instead, Joey was outside the nursery taking pictures and smiling.

"I brought you a change of clothes," Stacey said as she approached.

He eyed the bag and then her. A lopsided grin spread across his face. "You're the best. It was a rough night."

"Is everything okay with Rachel?"

"Oh yes. She was just fussy last night. The

nurses said she was probably getting used to the formula we're giving her." He took the bag from her outstretched hand and ushered her back toward Cameron's room. Stacey put the brakes on. She didn't want to go in there any more than she wanted to gouge her own eyeballs out of her head.

"Formula? I thought Cameron was feeding her until she went back to the prison."

"She did. The doctor gave the okay for her to be transferred back. They took her back this morning to the prison hospital. In the meantime, the nurses are giving me my own room until Rachel is clear to go home, which will be this time tomorrow."

Stacey started walking, mulling over all the information. "How did Cameron react when she had to leave?"

"The guards were nice and gave her a few minutes to say goodbye to Rachel. Afterwards, she seemed to be okay."

"Do you think...?" Stacey began but decided against it.

"Do I think she'll eventually want her back? I don't know. She'd be a fool if she didn't."

Stacey agreed. If the situation was reversed, she'd do all she could to get back to her baby. In the meantime, she'd enjoy whatever time God allowed her with Rachel and Joey.

"I missed you," Joey said, taking her hand in his and offering her a weak smile.

Stacey couldn't help but think those words were born from the fact Cameron was no longer there and he had no one else. Even if they were married, it didn't stop his heart from belonging to her. Seeing them in the delivery room together proved as much.

When she didn't say anything, he tugged her toward him. "Hey."

Giving him as big a smile as she dared without feeling fake, she asked, "What?"

"You okay? When you left yesterday I felt like there was a mountain between us."

The fake smile stayed plastered to her face. "No. Nothing was wrong. It's just all a little emotional for me." She looked down the hall to the hustle and bustle at the nurse's station and heard someone call that it was time for another baby to be born.

"Why did you snap at me? What's wrong with me calling you baby?"

"I don't like it. Plain and simple."

Joey studied her. Would he see right through to her soul and know she never wanted to be second best in his eyes? "Okay," he said slowly. "Can I give my wife a kiss?"

Stacey held in the frustrated sigh threatening to escape. Where did she fit in all this? Granted, Stacey could pinpoint the moment things got complicated: their wedding night. Before sex got involved, she could see clearly. She was there only for Rachel and to do a friend a favor. Give a baby a mother, give her childhood friend a wife so he could be more stable and raise his baby girl.

Then he'd gone and got her naked, the jerk. If she'd held tight to her original thoughts, a ring wouldn't be around her finger and the invisible noose around her neck. Could she live with Joey day after day with the memories in her mind of the way he'd looked and held Cameron?

Someone with a little more experience with men would know how to handle this. Maybe even suggest being adult enough to talk to him about it, but quite simply, Stacey was terrified to hear he could never love her and did, in fact, still love Cameron. It didn't take a rocket scientist to figure it out. They'd made a baby together for crying out loud.

Stacey leaned in and gave him a quick kiss on the cheek, but he grabbed her waist and hauled her to him, taking possession of her mouth. The bag she'd brought him with a change of clothes fell to the floor next to her foot, and his hand speared through her hair, bringing her closer.

His tongue delved deeply and his feral groan reminded her of their honeymoon, when he hadn't been able to get enough of her. Funny how things had changed the second they got back.

"Hey, whoa! We specialize in deliverin' babies here, not makin' 'em!" a dark-haired lady called out with a chuckle as she passed by with a rolling blood pressure monitor.

Joey tore away and pressed his forehead to hers. His embarrassed chuckle reminded her of the time they'd gotten caught behind his parents' shed, testing out what kissing felt like. Joey had heard a boy stuck his tongue in a girl's mouth when he really liked her. That had to have been about ten years ago now.

Boy, he'd figured it all out since then. Sadly, Stacey waited for about eleven more years before finding out for herself what boys did when they liked girls. She couldn't say it wasn't worth the wait, but she could have stood a little more preparation time and less complication. He'd gone and caught her off guard too many times.

"I can't wait to make love to you again, Stacey. All this…" he said, looking around him, "…it makes me want to shout with joy. It sounds so corny, but that baby in there is my life. I never thought I'd love her as much as I do. And I just want to celebrate her…and us."

Stacey sure did love being the afterthought. Pushing past her ridiculous and self-pitying subconscious, she gave him a smile. "Will you be home tonight?"

"Probably not. I'd like for you to stay with me, too. There are two beds in the room and you haven't even held her yet. I want you to bond with her the way I have."

Why did it feel so wrong? Like she was just a stand-in mother until the real one came along again.

Stacey tampered down the snort rising in her chest. It was exactly what she was. And she agreed to it, so she'd best buck up and take up the responsibility they'd agreed on.

"I don't think I can stay, Joey. I've got to go to the store and get a few necessities for her before you bring her home. She came a little early, remember? We don't have anything. No crib, no bassinet."

Joey pulled her into the room the nurses had given him and took out his wallet. "Here's my debit card. Buy whatever we need. I don't know anything about that stuff, so I'm giving you full reign."

Stacey turned the card over in her hands. "Sure."

"There's the newlyweds!" exclaimed Ms. McCrary as she flittered in and gathered them both in a hug. She held two massive gift bags which were weighted down. She sat them on the floor and blew a stray tendril out of her face.

"I've been shopping all morning! What kind of grandmother would I be if I didn't shower my beautiful granddaughter with all sorts of new stuff?"

"We were just talking about that," Stacey muttered. "I've got to get a few things today so we have a place to put her. We need a car seat, crib, bassinet, stroller…that's only the beginning."

"Well, I've got clothing, diapers, wipes, and newborn toys all taken care of right here." She patted the top of the bag and then started pulling tiny little outfits out, one by one. They were so small; Stacey could barely imagine a doll, let alone a human being fitting in them.

Ms. McCrary put a hand on top of hers and gave her a sympathetic frown. "I know it's all overwhelming, honey, but I'm here to help. Do you want me to go with you to pick out the crib and everything? I don't want to intrude, but I'm happy to go if you want me to."

"Actually, that sounds really good." Maybe she could help her keep things practical.

"Then it's settled. When we leave here, we'll hit all the baby stores in town and make my son earn some of his trust fund money."

Stacey laughed at the incredulous look on Joey's face. Then he narrowed his eyes at his mom and pointed a finger. "I have the granddaughter. I can hold her hostage if I need to."

Ms. McCrary laughed and held up her hands. "Fair enough. We'll be sensible, won't we, honey?"

Stacey looked at her mother-in-law and grinned when she winked at her. She could tell Joey was getting a kick out of watching the two of them together. But Stacey and his mom had always ganged up on him when they could and now was no exception.

"Here's the little woman of the hour!" a nurse exclaimed from the doorway as she wheeled in a plastic bassinet. "All vitals are good, Dad, and she's toasty warm. Just make sure to keep her fed every two hours."

Joey nodded and thanked the nurse. Then, as if he'd fathered twenty babies, he picked Rachel up with an expertise that left Stacey in awe and walked over to her. "Would you like to hold her?"

Stacey's emotions bounced back and forth for a few seconds. All the womanly instincts in her told her to grab the baby up and snuggle her and take care of her, but the insecure, less-experienced side of her balked.

"Let me!" Ms. McCrary exclaimed, jumping out of her seat and taking the baby. Whether by design or divine intervention, Stacey felt a tug of relief.

Joey sat next to her, confusion written

clearly in the frown of his eyebrows and the narrowing of his eyes. She knew him well enough to know he was trying to figure out what was wrong with her. Maybe later they would have a chance to talk, and she would get an opening to tell him how she felt. Of course, she didn't want him to think he had to take care of her, too. Walking on eggshells with your wife would be pretty difficult, especially when adjusting to a newborn in the house, too.

She watched her mother-in-law coo and giggle over the baby and every little movement she made. Stacey found herself craning her neck to take a peek. She hadn't seen her since the moment she came screaming into the world.

"Did you decide on a middle name?" Stacey asked, thinking about how they'd never discussed it.

"Rachel Hope. She's our hope that we'll eventually move forward with our lives."

Stacey stood and gathered her things. "I'm going to go ahead and get the stuff we need. Twenty-four hours will be here before we know it!"

Rushing to the door, she didn't realize Joey was close on her heels. He closed the door to the room, giving them some privacy.

"Something is wrong with you, and I want to know what it is." His tone brooked no argument. She looked into his blue eyes and immediately felt bad for ruining the memories of Rachel's birth.

"Can we just forget it, Joey? This is all overwhelming for me, okay. I'm not trying to ruin your day or your experience, I just don't know how to handle all this."

"Stacey," he began, his mouth working like he was searching for words. "I need you. I want you to love her as much as I do."

"And I will." It was a double-edged sword to tell him seeing him and Cameron together was hard, but she had to give him a little something to go on. "Joey…" She looked down the empty hallway, gathering her thoughts. "It was hard for me to see you with Cameron. I—"

"Stacey. You've always been a good friend to me, but you know I had a relationship with Cameron. She just had my kid. This marriage was never a love match and you know that." His face turned red and his arms flailed. "What am I supposed to do? Just stop all the feelings I ever had for her? Forget Rachel was a product of that?"

"Joey, it's not—" Stacey held her hands up to stop his rant. She recalled from childhood days he could easily get wound up on his own thoughts.

"Seeing her again brought it all back. I didn't want it to come back, but it did. I'm ready to move forward…and I have moved on. With you."

Stacey looked at the ground. "I saw her. She's beautiful. She's perfect for you. If you're having regrets about this, we can end it, Joey. I don't want it to get complicated."

Turning away from her and running his fingers through his hair, he let his arms fall with a big slap against his thighs. Then he spun back around. "It's already complicated, Stacey. I'm married to you. I have a baby with someone else. You're my best friend, but she was my lover. She's messed up; you're not. You confuse me out of my mind, Stacey. You're everything I didn't expect you to be. You're all grown up and… sexy. Way sexier than I ever thought you could be."

Stacey wasn't sure whether to be insulted or flattered. Instead, she got mad.

"I didn't go into this with expectations, but you know how I feel about you. How I've *always* felt about you. I love you, Joey, and maybe I jumped at the chance to be your wife just so I could have a little piece of what everyone else gets. Do you think I didn't want to be the one giving you a baby yesterday? Or be the one who hung the moon for you? Do you think I wanted to be the awkward third wheel in the delivery room when it was clear you love her so much? How easy do you think it was for a *wife* to watch, expectations or not?"

This seemed to make Joey come up short. "So now you're blaming me for something you agreed to?"

"No. I'm not blaming you. This is *my* fault. I should have never offered to get you out of your mess without knowing everything beforehand. Now an innocent baby is going to have to suffer because you couldn't keep your pants up."

Joey stooped nose to nose with her. "You're not being fair, and you know it."

Stacey closed her eyes and took a deep, cleansing breath. She wouldn't back down from him. Not now. "Isn't it the truth?"

"I loved her, Stacey. I still love her."

"I know you do. And I don't fault you for that. We can't help who we love sometimes. If I could, I wouldn't be here right now."

The truth of his statement weighed heavily on her as she turned to leave. She had agreed to do this because she loved Joey. It wasn't much of a surprise, but the reality of it saddened her. It was what her marriage was reduced to: loving someone who would never love her back. In some regards, she was okay with that, mainly because she didn't have to worry about herself as much. But then again, they had only been married for four days.

But it still left one major problem. The baby. If she was going to be a mother to her, she'd eventually have to buck up and at least hold her. Allow herself to feel.

However, Stacey had a job to do, and that was make sure her husband and his baby had somewhere to call home.

JOEY WAS in way over his head. His life was spiraling out of control. First, he'd gotten himself into a mess with Cameron, Stacey'd bailed him out of his mess, and now he was accountable to her. When he was more rational, he knew he owed her a lot more than he'd given her thus far. A few nights in bed with his wife, amazing as they were, didn't make everything okay.

He thought back about the delivery and how he'd stayed with Cameron. It wasn't something he'd first envisioned doing, or even knew if he'd be allowed to, but he was grateful for those few moments with Cameron again. A sober Cameron.

Even as he'd enjoyed his last few moments with her and watching their daughter being born, he'd wanted to share the moment with Stacey. The first minutes of Rachel's life had been a whirlwind, but once he'd turned, he'd wanted to spend those next minutes with Stacey. What did that tell him?

The same thing he'd always known: she was his friend. Maybe even his best friend. What other kind of person would do what she'd done for him if she wasn't a friend?

That night he decided to go home after all, and after saying his goodbyes to Rachel, he drove straight to the store and picked up some flowers for Stacey. It wasn't much, but it was a start.

As he walked through the door, he noticed a strong smell permeating the air. He followed his nose and found Stacey in short shorts. Her blonde, curly hair was pulled into a messy bun, and pink paint was smeared on her legs and cheek. She stood back, examining her handiwork. She was unbelievably adorable.

"Hey," he said quietly, holding out the daisies. Wielding a paintbrush, she spun around and smeared a little more paint across her cheek. He could tell she'd been crying.

"Hey," she greeted a little nasally. "You didn't have to do that." She nodded to the flowers.

"I know I didn't have to, but I wanted to. Can you take a break for a minute so we can talk?"

She examined the paint in her bucket and finally nodded. Walking past him, she headed to the kitchen without a word. As she washed her hands, he wasn't sure what to do or say so he stood there, still holding the flowers awkwardly.

"The color looks great. But are you sure you want her to use your grandfather's room?"

"It's the only room that makes sense. I just wish he was here to meet her." Turning, she leaned against the counter and dried her hands, the pure picture of domesticity.

"Me too. Listen, Stace, I owe you an apology. I was unfair today at the hospital. I think this whole situation has me a little emotional, too. I'm sorry for the things I said to you today."

Stacey's eyes fell downward, something he hated to see. He wanted her to look at him and fight, give him what he deserved. "You didn't say anything that wasn't the truth. And like you said, we were wide awake when we said our I do's."

He shuffled his feet. "But Stacey, I meant my vows. I meant in sickness and in health and good times and bad. I didn't vow it wouldn't be hard. Or we'd love each other immediately or even eventually. You told me you loved me today at the hospital, but you don't know me. It's like you said, you love the idea of me and what you've never had. I did things in college I'm not proud of. I hate no one has ever appreciated you the way you deserve, and if I was standing on the outside looking in, I'd punch myself in the face."

This brought a smile to her lips.

"I want to love you the way you deserve. Maybe I don't feel what you feel right now, but I will respect you. You've made a lot of sacrifices for me, and I appreciate it. And I love you as my best friend and I always will."

"I don't think that'll be enough, Joey. I'm just trying to be honest here. I got into this thinking I could stay unemotional, but the second we had sex on our honeymoon, my emotions kicked into overdrive. It's not fair for you to be saddled with me when I clearly can't control my feelings."

"I'm not saddled with you. I don't want you to ever feel that way." He placed the flowers on the kitchen table and took her in his arms. "You're proving to be the kind of wife I've always dreamed of having. Someone who puts the kids and me first, someone who does all they can to make sure we have a home. Now that Rachel's coming home in the morning, it's time for me to put you first. I know Rachel will need me, but when it comes to emotional support, you're gonna be sick of me."

Stacey smiled. "I think we've established I'm a pretty big sucker when it comes to you, Joey."

"Sucker enough to kiss me?"

Stacey grinned and pecked him on the

cheek.

"That's all you've got for me? I've been starving for you, honey."

As his lips descended, Stacey turned her head. "Joey, I'm not going to say this isn't difficult. Seeing you with Cameron was a hard pill to swallow."

His grip relaxed on her and he pressed his forehead to hers. "I've been thinking about things, and I was wrong."

"You don't have to explain anything to me. I just want you to look me in the eye and tell me it's not her you're thinking about when you're kissing me."

Joey felt like he could cry. Had he made her feel that way? He was such a failure at being a husband not even four days into it. The good news was he was going to change things. Starting now.

Stacey was an amazing, selfless woman whom he loved dearly. Carefully, he touched her collarbone and traced the delicate curves there. "Stacey," he whispered. "If there's one thing I'm sure about, it's the fact it's all you I'm touching. No one else feels as good as you do." He surprised himself by realizing he spoke the truth. To demonstrate his words, he slipped his hands under the hem of her shirt and touched her belly. The subtle intake of breath told him she was well aware of his intentions.

"And there's no one else I want to kiss other than you, Stacey." His lips found her jaw and he trailed his mouth along her skin. "And the best part?"

"Mmm?" she rasped.

"There's no one else I want touching me." He guided her hands to his chest and watched her fingers flex over him. But apparently it wasn't enough. She tugged at his shirt, and he granted her request by pulling his shirt over his head. "Are you okay with this? Doing this here?"

Stacey pulled back and gave him a staggering smile that left him reeling at the sweetness. "The idea has grown on me today. What kind of wife would I be if I denied you the one thing we have in common?"

"What's that?" He watched her fiddle with his pants button, her shyness more of a turn-on than seeing her in leather holding a whip.

"We love having sex."

Joey took the opportunity to press against her. "This isn't just sex, Stacey. I don't have sex with my wife, I make love to her."

Pink flushed her cheeks as she looked away.

"What, you don't believe me?"

"I never said that. It's just that you *don't* love me."

"I love you in all the ways that matter."

Stacey would need to get over this low self-esteem and quick. He knew her background and knew she was inexperienced, but there really wasn't any need to be. Her blonde curly hair alone was enough to drive him mad, but coupled with her green eyes and her slender frame, he was amazed he was able to function. And getting to know her slowly, seeing her routines and her kind soul made her even more attractive.

"Come with me," he whispered, determined to prove to her what he saw.

Together they walked down the hallway. After pulling Stacey into their bedroom, he yanked her to him and pressed his mouth to hers. A small whimper and her hands clutching at his pants again drove him mad. But before he took his wife, she would see what he saw.

Joey worked what Cameron had once called "magic" and made sure she was ready for him. He slowly peeled the clothes away from her body, and when she was naked, he moved Stacey across the room where the floor length mirror on the back of the door was mounted. He closed the door and spun around to look into the mirror.

"Look at yourself, Stacey."

Immediately, she cringed and tried to turn, but he held her steady.

"Look at yourself. Look at what I see."

Dipping his head, he nibbled on her throat until she squirmed again. "Look at yourself," he urged. "Open your eyes."

When she did what he asked, he slipped his hand around to her stomach, touching her slowly. "Your skin is so soft," he whispered. "I could touch you all day."

"Joey…"

"Look at your skin, Stacey. Look how porcelain it is, like a china doll. Do you know how rare that is? It's like you're untouched and pure."

"I was before I married you. You went and ruined me on our wedding night."

He grinned. "Once we're done here, I'm going to taint you again…and again…and again."

"Why don't we just skip to the good part?" She squirmed against him. He couldn't lose his resolve now.

"But your skin isn't all I love."

She sighed.

"Hear me out." He ran his hands up and down her side, feeling her curves and the thin layer of perspiration. He loved knowing she was hot for him.

"Joey, this isn't necessary."

"Oh, but it is. And I'm going to point out something I love about you every single time I catch you being embarrassed about praise someone gives you." Repositioning himself, he reached up and pulled her hair loose out of the ponytail holder. It fell down in a spiraled heap, like tiny winding staircases. It wasn't the frizzy curly he'd seen on other girls but rather the type of curls girls tried for on prom day or on their wedding.

"I love your hair."

Stacey rolled her eyes.

"I *love* your hair," he insisted and buried his nose in it. "It smells like grapes. It always has. I remember when we were kids, and you tried straightening it once. I was so mad. You're not my Stacey without curly hair."

"It's a mess."

"It's beautiful, Stace. It's like honey. When you wear it up, it reminds me of a halo."

Stacey snorted. "Got you fooled, huh?"

"Not at all. I know underneath your halo is a set of horns that comes out when we're naked."

A giggle erupted from her chest. Her smile was his trophy.

"And your smile? Wow, Stacey. It was the first thing I noticed when you were playing with your friend across the street. You girls were playing together and whispering. Then you threw your head back and laughed, and I was lost. I stood there like a dope waiting for you to do it again." His hands slid up her back and massaged.

"Then we moved out back because some creeper was staring at us across the street?"

"Pretty much." He grinned at her reflection in the mirror. "And those green eyes? Enough to melt me, and I do every time you look at me. When you get all aroused, did you know your pupils dilate? Your lids close a little, and while I know you're with me, it's like you're somewhere deep inside your mind, taking all the pleasure I can give you."

"Great. So I look drunk?"

"Oh yeah, and that's not a bad thing. Cause I know I made you that way without a drop of alcohol." Unable to take it anymore, he kissed her on her shoulder, nipping it before moving his hands up to touch her breasts.

"And these. The Bible even speaks of how these will bring me pleasure."

"My body is yours, Joey."

"They're perfect. Just right."

"Anything more than a handful is a waste anyway, right?"

It was hard to keep a straight face, but he somehow managed. "Nothing about you is a waste."

"Make love to me, Joey," she pleaded, her voice raspy and soft.

"Oh, I will. When I'm done."

Their eyes locked in the mirror, and his

hands slid down, back to her hips. "Did you know hips are the sexiest part of the body to me?"

"Awesome. I don't have any."

"*Au contraire*, my lady, what is this?" He bent down and kissed the curve of her hip, slightly less defined than the rest of her, but certainly no less sexy. She was what some might call lanky as she was tall and slender, but seeing her without clothes on was a whole new treat for him.

"And this?" He moved to the other side and placed a tender kiss there. Her skin scorched his lips. "These legs, Stacey. These legs are enough to make me want to lock you away for no one else to see."

"I do have great legs, don't I?" She grinned.

He looked up at her and wiggled his eyebrows appreciatively as his hands roamed her legs.

"Too bad they end with ski feet."

"Ski feet?"

She stuck a foot out and waggled her toes. "Boat feet, ski feet, clod hoppers, Sasquatch. The list goes on."

"For heaven's sake, Stacey," he said and couldn't hold it in any longer. He gave a big belly laugh.

Immediately she turned red and turned in the direction of her clothes.

"No no. Do you have any clue why I'm laughing?"

"I suspect it hasn't something to do with whatever is between my hips and my toes."

"I'm laughing because it's so ridiculous. You find a way to ruin everything I see in you."

"I'm sorry."

"Don't be sorry. Just say thank you! Believe that *I* believe you're beautiful! Could I keep it up if I wasn't attracted to you?"

A blush singed her cheeks this time. "Only if you were thinking of Cameron."

Frustrated, he took her face between his hands. "You are Stacey McCrary. My *wife*. My friend. My lover. Cameron is history because I have you." He spun her around to face the mirror again. "Tell me what you like about yourself other than your legs."

"That's about it."

"Think harder."

Stacey looked at her body and finally mumbled, "I guess I like my flat stomach."

"Okay, what else?" Now they were getting somewhere.

"My smile is okay. My parents bought me braces when I was a teenager."

"I remember." He gave her a knowing smile, thinking of the time he'd teased her about not kissing another boy with braces or they'd lock together. She'd been mortified enough she'd believed him. It was how he'd convinced her to try kissing him first. "Look in the mirror and tell me how beautiful you are."

"You know I can't, Joey."

"Do it for me. And because you'll put us both out of our misery, and we can get down to business."

Slowly, her eyes rose from her feet to her face's reflection. "I'm beautiful," she said flatly.

"Great start! Now say it like you mean it."

Stacey eyed him suspiciously. "What's in this for you?"

"Absolutely nothing other than seeing you happy with yourself. Now say it like you mean it." To get her back in the game, he placed a hot-mouthed kiss on her neck and used his tongue to swirl lazy patterns along her skin. "Say it," he said against her ear when he was done with her neck.

"I'm beautiful," she whispered, pushing against him like a cat needing a good rub.

"Again," he urged, wrapping his arms around her and pulling her close.

"I'm beautiful."

"God made you beautiful, Stacey. And all this is mine. He gave it to me the day we said I do. And to say you're not beautiful is scoffing in God's face. To tell me I'm lying about how I feel is scoffing in my face. One day you're going to wake up and realize how right we are. Maybe not right now, but soon. And when you do, I'm going to take you in my arms," he turned her to face him, away from the mirror, "and I'm going to look you square in the face and say I told you so." Joey grinned at Stacey, and he was happy to see she returned his smile just as his lips crashed down on hers, and he proved to her just how beautiful they could be together.

CHAPTER ELEVEN

THE DAY JOEY and Stacey brought Rachel home from the hospital was a sunny day. The weather was turning from hot and humid to rainy and comfortable. Stacey had lost her papa in August, and it was now late September. Fall was just around the corner.

With Rachel fast asleep in her car seat, Stacey poured them both a glass of sweet tea and joined him in the living room. Joey didn't want to remove her for fear of waking her up. Stacey still needed to take on the difficult task of holding her and learning how to take care of her. But she imagined it couldn't be much different than taking care of her grandfather…

They sat across from each other in silence in the living room, and Joey eyed her. "Last night was pretty awesome, huh?" he asked with a half grin.

Stacey grinned and focused on wiggling her toes. "Yes."

"We're both gonna be pretty tired for the next few months. I'm gonna miss having you all to myself."

She glanced up at him. "But we have Rachel now, and she's a blessing." Despite her words, she eyed the tiny baby and wondered if she would make or break their marriage. She certainly had Cameron's pretty face and a dimple on her right cheek. Every time Joey looked at her, it would remind him of Cameron and all they had.

But maybe they could get past it. With time. Time could take away everything, even the feelings Joey had for his ex-lover. But would time grant him the love she so longed from him?

Stacey watched as Joey shook his head. "Would you relax? I know what you're thinking."

"What am I thinking?" she challenged quietly.

"The same thing you were thinking last night. But I'm not going to go back to Cameron and forget all about you. Have you ever realized when things get bad, you're the first person I always come to?"

Stacey tried to take it as the compliment it was meant to be. "Yes, I've noticed."

"I trust you, Stace. More than anyone. And I hope you know how much I trust you to raise my daughter with me. I might have loved Cameron, but I don't think I would have given such blind trust to her. She had a lot to prove to me after the things she put me through."

"I'm glad you feel that way about me," she murmured. She *was* glad. In her world, trust did equal love. Love wasn't some overpowering emotion he seemed to be looking for. It was quiet, steady and always there. Maybe she'd been looking at things from all the wrong angles. A surge of happiness swept through her. It would just take him time. She thought of all the summer days they'd spent together in their youth, building their relationship and their friendship. Even as young kids, there had been something between them that always seemed to bring them back together.

Maybe it was up to her to show him what love really was. And real love didn't play games like Cameron had.

Standing, she walked over to him and sat in his lap. Surprise registered on his handsome face, but he placed his glass of tea on the table next to him and put his arms around her, pulling her close. She kissed him slowly, loving the way he responded to her. His soft exhale told her all she needed to know.

"We have a baby," she whispered as she pulled away. A smile crept across her face, the awe of God's little miracle finally hitting her full force.

Joey studied her for a moment, like he didn't believe her. But then a full-fledged smile caught her, and she couldn't look away. "We do have a baby. A beautiful one. And one day? Lord willing, it'll be you giving birth to my next baby. But right now, I want to focus on our marriage and making sure we stay on the right path. There's just something about this…about you…it feels right. I can't explain it. If you'd have asked me six months ago where I'd be today, I probably would have shrugged."

Stacey kissed his cheek and ran her fingers through his dark hair. "We'll have fun or die trying."

Joey didn't smile. Instead, his steady gaze gave her the distinct impression he was about to say something monumental.

"I'm so happy with you, Stacey. My heart is full of it."

Yes, Stacey was right to start looking at things from a different angle. Joey's eyes shone with love and joy. Now it was just waiting for him to realize something that was already a part of him. She'd wait forever if she had to.

Right in front of her, his eyes grew bright and watery, another testament to how strong his emotions were. Stacey didn't want to wait for any more words. She leaned in and kissed him deeply. She held nothing back, but instead gave him everything, resolving to herself and to God she wouldn't feel sorry for her situation anymore or give him a reason to wish for Cameron. It would take some time to get over being so shy around him and looking at him in a different light, but she *would* do it. It couldn't be fun hanging around someone who was constantly putting herself down. Even she got tired of hearing herself.

Joey pulled her closer, his hands squeezing and roaming over her body. Beneath her, he squirmed and adjusted so she straddled him. Stacey was pretty sure she was about to implode when a tiny squeak caused her to go rigid and pull away. Joey followed her, his eyes glazed with passion as he continued kissing her neck and moving against her.

"Joey," she whispered. She shot a glance over her shoulder and confirmed that, indeed, Rachel was awake. Two dark blue orbs stared straight ahead as she wiggled and squeaked again.

"She's awake," she said again, this time a little louder.

"Mmm," Joey murmured, pulling her

mouth down for another hot kiss.

When a cry pierced the room, Stacey jerked back again. "Joey, I think she's hungry."

"I'm hungry, too," he growled in her ear.

"No. The baby. Rachel is hungry. Your daughter!" Desperation filled her when she realized she had no willpower to move away from him.

"Just a second," he whispered and put his hot lips on her bare stomach. He'd lifted her shirt at some point and now her focus was everywhere but on the squirming, fussing baby.

How did people do this? It amazed her the population wasn't triple what it was. If Joey continued, he'd have her pregnant with a single one of his lusty looks.

"Okay, Joey, I'm pulling the plug." Gathering all of her wits, she stood away from him, grabbed his hands, and placed them in his lap.

"Stace, c'mon. She's fine."

Stacey smiled. "But in about two seconds, she won't be. Why don't you fix her bottle, and I'll hold her. I haven't made it a point yet, and I'd like to get to know her."

His vision sharpening, he looked at her with a little bit of doubt. "Are you sure?"

She didn't have to think twice. With a nod, she walked over and unbuckled Rachel. As she pulled the baby out, she arched her back and her tiny fists came up next to her cheeks as she stretched. Stacey smiled and folded her arms around her. The feel of the baby in her arms was unlike anything she'd ever felt before. This was *her* baby to raise with the man she loved. Rachel was *hers*.

Cradling Rachel, Stacey rubbed her palm over her downy hair. She could see the pulsing spot on her head and awed over God's creation. Rachel looked up at her with those big blue eyes and smacked her mouth. Turning her head to the side, she rooted toward Stacey's arm. When she found nothing, her face crumpled.

Stacey looked up to see what was taking Joey so long but found him standing in the doorway watching her with a warm look across his features.

"I didn't think I could get any happier, Stace. You're gonna be a great mother."

With that, he turned around and disappeared into the kitchen. Stacey smiled and looked down at Rachel. It was one thing she didn't have to worry about. She *would* be a great mother.

IT WAS ON the tip of his tongue. *I love you.* Three simple words that meant so much. Three simple words that could destroy her if he was wrong and only caught up in the emotions of the moment. Three simple words he didn't understand and was afraid to figure out.

Because it meant inevitable pain. Just look at where it had gotten him with Cameron. But would lightning really strike twice? Could two women who were so completely different break his heart the same way? Surely if this feeling was love, it wouldn't go away. That's why he'd held himself back. He wanted to make sure it wasn't just him being in the moment.

Something had changed between them today. He wasn't sure what it was…maybe the fact she'd initiated physical contact first or seemed happier with Rachel home, but he wasn't going to look a gift horse in the mouth. He had his best friend, now his lover, and a wonderful woman to call his wife. There was no doubt in his mind Cameron would have fallen pathetically short at domestic bliss. She wasn't the type to settle down and stay in one place for long.

Then there was Stacey. Sweet, predictable Stacey who was always there for him no matter what. Always bailing him out of his problems. Only this time, it was something he could never repay. He could certainly try, but it would never be enough.

As he shook the bottle of milk, he couldn't help but smile. He hadn't lied when he said he was happy. It wasn't just the happiness either. He was content. If nothing ever changed for him again, he'd never have a reason to be unhappy. He had everything he'd ever wanted.

A piercing wail snapped him out of his reverie, and he hurried to Stacey with the bottle. The crying baby didn't even seem to rattle her. She already had a burp cloth slung over her shoulder and Rachel poised to eat. She might be shy and awkward but with a baby in her arms, she was beautiful and perfect. A total natural.

Beaming down at Rachel, Stacey slipped the bottle into the baby's mouth and smiled. It was one of those moments Joey wanted to remember forever. Silently moving back to the chair across the room, he worked his cell phone out of his pocket and took a picture of the moment he'd remember the rest of his life.

The fake cha-chink of the shutter on the phone caused Stacey to look up.

"What are you doing?" she asked with a grin.

"Remembering how special the two women in my life are."

Stacey's eyes seemed to involuntarily go back to Rachel's face. "She's so beautiful," she murmured.

"I know." But he wasn't looking at his baby.

Rachel held Stacey's pinky as she slurped

down the bottle. After a few moments, she put the bottle on the table and held her up against her shoulder and patted her back.

For a moment, she simply inhaled Rachel's baby smell, her eyes closed and a soft look relaxing her features. Then Stacey rubbed her cheek against her downy head. It was almost enough to make a grown man cry. Joey shifted in his seat and swallowed past the lump in his throat.

When Stacey's gaze focused on him, her eyes were sparkling. "I think I already love her," she whispered, a single tear rolling down her cheek.

Joey swallowed again, knowing in his heart Stacey was the only woman for him. "Me, too."

CHAPTER TWELVE

The next few weeks went by in a sleepy haze as one day ran into the next. Rachel might have been small, but she was mighty when she was hungry or dirty. Stacey had fallen into a nice routine, but she was exhausted.

Exhaustion didn't cover the powerful emotions of loving someone. Rachel was just as much her child as she was Cameron's. She might have come from Cameron's body, but Stacey was the woman raising the baby, and she was determined to do it well. So far, so good. Rachel was on a predictable schedule—thanks to the aid of several books on sleep training. She was already sleeping about six hours at night.

Because Joey was back at work, she tried to make sure he didn't get up with her much during the night. Even so, he wanted to get up on the weekends and watch her. Stacey admired how easily fatherhood came to him. She enjoyed Rachel, but sometimes she felt like a pretender. Joey was vocal about what a natural she was, and she was learning slowly but surely. It was just not as fast as she'd hoped.

It was Friday and Joey's mom had offered to take Rachel for the night so they could catch up on their sleep. When Stacey saw her crossing the street to come get the baby, she felt relief wash over her. Rachel had been fussy most of the day, and she hadn't sat down, save a handful of times. When was the last time she'd eaten?

Ms. McCrary chirped a hello as she pushed the door open and clapped her hands together when her eyes landed on Rachel.

"Warning, she's a fussy pants today." Stacey handed the baby over and promptly plopped on the seat behind her.

"A fussy pants? No way!" The woman bounced, and Rachel immediately calmed and studied her grandmother's face. The string of coos and nonsense coming out of her mouth made Stacey chuckle.

"She's a charmer."

Ms. McCrary looked her over for a split

second. "One of those days, huh? You look exhausted."

"I am."

"You know, I could come over more and help you. It's not like I'm busy now that I've retired. If you're having a bad day, at least bring her to me for a couple of hours so you can recoup."

"That's okay. This is what I signed on for. But you know you're more than welcome to visit her anytime."

She continued bouncing even though Rachel's eyes were drifting shut. "How're things between you and Joey?"

"Good." She smiled when she thought of her husband and his amazing patience. "He's wonderful."

"You're pretty great, too, ya know."

"I just never want him to regret his decision to marry me. I love Rachel as much as he does now."

"You think he would divorce you and take her away if you guys were in a fight?"

"No." Stacey waved a dismissal hand in front of her. "We just rushed into things. I don't want to overwhelm him with my neediness." In a classic gesture, she pushed up her glasses and sniffed.

"You're not needy. You're the most selfless person I've ever met, Stacey. How many other women would want to do this for a friend?"

She looked down with a frown. "You know he's more than a friend. I love him."

"And he loves you. He'll see that eventually. That boy has loved you since you had pigtails and were riding a tricycle."

Stacey smiled, knowing the words were true. But was it enough? How did Cameron play into all this? What if she ever came back?

"I know he does in his own way," Stacey admitted. It felt good to say it out loud.

"Did he tell you he has to go to court next week?"

She nodded. "Yes. DHR is coming to check our home situation on Monday, too."

Ms. McCrary's mouth fell into a grim line. "I know you'll pass with flying colors. I already see a huge change in Joey, and I know you and Rachel have played a huge part in helping him grow up in the last few months."

Stacey looked outside to the brilliant fall colors. It was almost Halloween. Then the holiday season would come upon them full force, and she'd finally get to experience what it was like to be part of a real family. Not that Papa hadn't given her enough. But ever since her parents had died, she'd missed the camaraderie between family members. A gaping hole had been torn open and never quite filled the same way after they'd died. Papa could only do so much in his old age.

"Do you have her bags packed? Of course, I know where you live if I need something." She laughed at her own joke.

Stacey rolled her eyes. She stood up again, her back and feet screaming at her. "They're in her room, let me get them."

When she returned with the bags, her mother-in-law already had Rachel strapped in the car seat sound asleep.

"I would love to know how you do it." Stacey sighed, looking at the sleeping beauty.

"It's not something you get until you're past your child-bearing years. Mine never did this, either. I guess you could call it a grandmother skill."

The two women grinned. "Thank you for taking her tonight. It'll be nice to get a good night's sleep."

"And for you and Joey to have a night alone. I know having a baby four days after getting married isn't typically ideal."

"No, but we're dealing. We fit each other in where we can."

"That's not a great way to start a marriage," she said sternly.

"I know. When she's a bit bigger we'll have more time."

Ms. McCrary studied her then turned. "Just call me when you guys wake up in the morning.

I'll keep her as long as you need me to."

Stacey stood in her living room and looked around. Bottles everywhere. Rolled up dirty diapers she needed to throw away were strewn strategically by the bassinet. With a sigh, Stacey resolved to do some power cleaning before Joey came home from work. She knew if she sat down, she'd be gone in thirty seconds flat.

JOEY WAS LOOKING forward to a night alone with Stacey. It would be their first since Rachel was born. Joey was starved for his wife, and he planned to make good use of their time alone.

Walking in from a long day at work, he immediately noticed the smell of cleaning supplies and frowned. She was cleaning? The house was already spotless. Sure enough, as he glanced around, he saw the dishes were done, the table set, dinner in the oven and heard the golden silence, save some scrubbing coming from the bathroom.

He found Stacey on her knees, gloves on, wielding a toilet brush.

"Hey, Supergirl."

She smiled her knee-melting smile and rolled her eyes. "I knew if I sat down I'd be out for the count."

"Isn't that the goal of Mom taking her?"

"Well, it needed to be done. And I don't want to just sleep tonight. Although it is on the agenda." She cocked an eyebrow at him, and he was pretty sure there wasn't another woman on this planet who could look sexy while scrubbing a toilet.

"How long until dinner's ready?" he asked, sweat beading on his forehead. It had been days since he'd enjoyed his wife, and he was ready to get to the good stuff.

"About an hour." Replacing the toilet brush and flushing, she removed her gloves slowly as she stalked over to him.

Her short shorts gave him enough of a view to leave his mouth watering. He loved her legs, loved them even more when they were wrapped around his waist. Her hair was in that messy updo he loved so much, with little spiral tendrils escaping and teasing her temples.

"An hour, huh?" He swallowed down some air at the look in her eyes. Sheer naughtiness.

"Mmm-hmm."

When she reached him, she wasted no time wrapping her arms around his shoulders and kissing his neck. She trailed kisses up to his ear and finally whispered, "C'mon, Superman, let me show you how to fly."

During dinner, Joey had a hard time keeping his hands to himself. Just when he thought Stacey couldn't surprise him anymore after a dinner filled with excessive touching and heated looks, she went and proved him wrong. Cameron had been the aggressor many times, but up until a few hours ago, Stacey had been content to be submissive. But not that evening. She'd used him for pleasure, pleasured him and then told him exactly what she wanted after dinner. He'd been shocked little Stacey Ingram could be so explicit, but he was happy he'd never have to guess with her.

She slanted her green eyes his way. "Will you stop it? We've got all night."

"Uh, I don't know about you but I plan to sleep at least part of the night. Mom would be disappointed in us if we didn't take her up on her offer."

"Your mother would be tickled pink we're making good use of our time. It was probably part of her plan anyway."

"Regardless. We're both exhausted."

"Agreed. But I do miss the little booger."

"Knowing she's just across the street helps me. I get the best of both worlds. You and knowing my baby is close by."

Stacey took a bite of her roll and then set it down. She took his hand in hers and looked away.

"What is it?" he asked, suddenly alarmed. She'd gone from a minx to a shy little kitten, her eyes never quite meeting his.

"I just want to say something."

"Go on." He wanted to wrap her in his arms and never let go. He hated to see her so unsure about saying something to him.

She fidgeted for a moment and finally those green, soulful eyes looked into his. "I love you."

It was probably the last thing he expected to hear. She clearly misread the intake of air on his end.

"I know you don't love me, okay? I *know* it. But I just want to tell you I love you. Maybe I can love enough for the both of us, but either way, I don't want to hide it anymore. Not that I could." Again, her eyes cast downward. "I've loved you since we were little. And now? Being married to you and helping you raise your daughter… it's a little surreal. I love who you are on the inside. I love how you make me feel. And I love how we are together. At first I was a little confused about things and maybe even a little resentful, but now I know things happen for a reason. Rachel has a mother now. And I have a life I wouldn't have gotten otherwise."

Joey stared at her in disbelief. Did she really think she wasn't worthy of marriage? "Stace…"

"You don't have to say anything. I don't really *want* you to say anything. I just want you to know I love you. That's all."

Joey exhaled and studied his fingers. He wanted to say it to her. How much surer of things did he need to be with her? He'd married her. He'd asked her to raise his daughter. He'd made love to her.

"Stace?" The lump in his throat choked him. He prayed he wasn't about to make a horrible decision.

"Let me get this table cleaned off and we can get back to business." She snatched her hands from his and gathered their plates. But Joey was too quick for her.

"Sit."

She did as she was told, the plates making a loud clang against the wooden table.

"Stacey."

"What, Joey?"

Now he knew why she could never look at him during the important conversations. The insecurity had the power to undo him if he let it. He didn't want to read her rejection or her doubt of his next words. She might love him, but would she believe him?

He concentrated on a speck in the wood grain and frowned. He felt a headache coming on from the tensed muscles and he rubbed his forehead for some relief.

Finally, as if the weight of the world had drained from him, he looked up and said it. "I love you, too, Stacey."

Silence.

And more silence.

Chancing her fury, he cocked an eyebrow at her and saw tears had welled in her eyes. He wasn't sure if they were happy tears or angry tears.

"I love you, Stacey," he said again, wondering if she'd even heard him.

"I heard you…" She looked past him and blinked slowly, pushing the tears out of her eyes and down both cheeks simultaneously. She cleared her throat. "Are you sure?"

"I think so."

"You think so or you know so?" Her intense study of his face made him feel like a slide under a microscope. He knew she would be able to see everything.

"I know so. I've loved you since we were little kids, too."

"How do you know you love me?"

Joey let out a quick exhale and smiled. Leave it to a woman to need an explanation. "I just do. You bring out the best in me. I feel like a teenager again when I'm with you. And you're my best friend. Always have been."

Stacey grinned, seemingly satisfied with what she saw in his face. "That makes me really happy, Joey. More than I could ever tell you."

She leaned her head on his shoulder and

swiped at the tears.

"Please tell me those are happy tears," he said, lifting her chin with his index finger, forcing her gaze to meet his.

"Of course they're happy tears. I never thought I'd hear you say that to me."

"There's nothing about you I don't love, Stacey. I love your lips…" He kissed her mouth. "I love your neck and the way you put on just enough perfume to entice me." He placed an open mouth kiss on her neck. "Come to bed with me, Stacey. Let's make love."

Stacey's hands came up and framed his face. She reverently touched his lips and his jawline, her fingertips soft and inviting. "I'd like that," she whispered. Her quirked lips undid him. In less than two seconds, he swept her up into his arms and carried her down the hallway.

CHAPTER THIRTEEN

"So the DHR rep said everything looked good?" Stacey asked as she folded tiny socks together.

"Yup. We passed with flying colors. Things should be moving along with the court systems to make sure she's officially ours." Joey placed a kiss on top of her head as he walked by, getting Rachel's bottle ready.

"What's next?" She stopped for a moment to see his reaction.

He ran his fingers through his hair. "I have to convince Cameron to sign her over permanently. The lawyer says she's being quiet about everything right now, which probably isn't good."

"You know her better than any of us. Is she going to get out and take her back?" Panic seized her chest, and she exhaled, trying to calm her nerves.

"It's okay, Stacey. We'll fight for her if we have to. She'll know how much we love her."

"When is Cameron up for parole?"

"In eleven months."

By Rachel's first birthday. What a nice birthday present, to be handed over to someone she didn't even know. But maybe it wouldn't happen if Stacey prayed hard enough.

"Can you give Rachel her bottle while I finish up these clothes? I'll put her down afterwards."

"I kinda of want to put her down tonight. Do you mind?" Joey asked with a little grin.

"By all means."

"Why don't you go put on something sexy for me while I'm playing Mr. Mom."

Stacey grinned at him. He was so cute in the evenings, when all was quiet and peaceful. Sometimes they snuggled, sometimes they made love, other times they just watched TV or got into a deep conversation about religion or God.

Stacey had to admit her faith had been put on the back burner since getting married. Sure, she still prayed, but her daily Bible readings had been put on hold. One day, she'd like to read the Bible with Joey since he'd admitted before they got married he liked to read the Bible, too.

Later that night, as she lay in bed listening to Joey's soft breath as he slept, she wondered what their life would be like when Cameron was out of prison. Eleven months wasn't enough with her sweet baby girl, and she needed to know she had more time to be a mother.

Joey said he loved her. Was quick to show her, too. But out of sight was sometimes out of mind and that's what she feared the most with Cameron. If she was to show up again, how would Joey handle it?

Over the monitor, Stacey heard Rachel stirring. She slept longer stretches now that she was a few weeks old, but Stacey found she loved the feedings during the night and her unique time with her. There was something special about having her all to herself, knowing her husband was sleeping in the next room. It had taken a while, but Stacey had finally bonded with her, and she couldn't imagine her life without her.

As Stacey settled in to feed Rachel, she heard Joey's cell phone ring. Who could be calling him at one in the morning?

Rachel sucked contentedly on her bottle. Stacey stood carefully and went to the door, trying to hear who he was speaking to.

"Cameron, why are you calling at one in the morning?"

Stacey allowed a small gasp to escape. Her worst fear was on the other end of the line.

"No, I'm not with her. Stacey's feeding her right now. What do you need?"

Again, Stacey strained her ears to hear what he was saying. He spoke softly, no doubt trying to hide his conversation. Stacey couldn't blame him, but she also wanted to scream at the craziness of their situation.

"Let me get this straight. You're calling me at one in the morning to tell me some sob story about how much you miss me? Cameron, Please. You've made your choice, and I've made mine."

Stacey straightened a little.

"No, it wasn't a mistake. Your daughter has a mother she wouldn't have had otherwise. So no, I didn't make a mistake. You're the one who made the mistake. If you hadn't screwed up so royally, we might still be together and be raising her together."

And just like that, Stacey deflated.

"Yes, I've told her I love her."

She waited with her ear next to the door, waiting to see what he said next.

"No, I *do* love her. She's an amazing woman…No, she's not you, but she's so much better in so many ways."

It was like watching a train wreck, Stacey decided. She couldn't back away from the door.

"My sex life is none of your business anymore," he issued harshly.

She heard him give a low chuckle. "Yes, we had some great nights together. But they're over. I'm married, and I'm happy. Rachel's happy."

Stacey was happy if he was happy. But would it be enough?

"You should see her, Cam. She started smiling a few days ago. She looks just like you."

Stacey glanced in the darkness down at Rachel. Her eyes were drifting shut as her tummy filled.

"I'd have to talk to Stacey about bringing her. I'm not sure how she would feel about it...Yes, I know you're her mother, but you also made a lot of bad choices that took rights away from you, at least until you can straighten up when you get out."

Stacey's eyes slammed shut. She wanted to see Rachel, which couldn't be a good thing. Sitting in a cell all day gave her the opportunity to think about her choices, and that, above all else, scared her. She knew Joey wouldn't have the heart to say no to her.

When Rachel finished, Stacey burped her and put her back down. She drifted right back to sleep with her little fists curled above her head. Stacey smiled, enjoying the moments she knew would be fleeting, whether from taking their time together for granted over the coming years or from Cameron demanding visitation.

Stacey padded into the room and slipped under the covers. Joey immediately came to her side of the bed and pulled her into his arms.

Swallowing thickly, she asked, "Who was on the phone?"

"Oh, no one. Just a wrong number."

With a great jab, Stacey's heart slammed into her ribcage. He'd lied to her! How could he possibly lie after everything she'd done for him?

Raising up, Stacey looked him in the eyes, ready to fight.

"I love you, Stace," he said before she could speak. He trailed his thumb over her lips. If she'd been a little stronger, she could have resisted him, but she wasn't. The tenderness in his eyes warred with the words still in her head.

When she didn't say anything, he took this as an opportunity to kiss her tenderly. Stacey really wanted to bite him as hard as she could, but she refrained and selfishly enjoyed the moment.

He finally pulled away and smiled at her sleepily, then hauled her back into his arms, holding her close.

Stacey chose to keep silent. There was no

telling when all of this would be taken away from her, and she wanted to make sure she had plenty of memories to look back on when Joey's side of the bed was cold and empty.

JOEY HAD LIED to her. How could he have done that to his wife? A woman who'd given up everything to help him with a situation he'd put himself in!

That was just it, though. She hadn't felt like she was giving anything up. She felt like she was cornered and Joey was her only shot at having a happily ever after. He'd give anything to take the moment back. To not answer his phone. To not engage Cameron in a wistful trip down memory lane on their sex life.

Cameron might have been more adventurous in bed, but Stacey was sexy and the emotion between them surpassed anything he and Cameron shared.

Still though, and this was the part that killed him to admit, it had felt good to hear Cameron's voice. She'd called him often in the middle of the night when they were dating. At the time, he'd thought she'd been lying in bed thinking of him and had decided to come over. Now he knew with the power of hindsight she'd been out doing drugs, and he'd been a convenient place to rest her head as she came down off her high.

In ways, he'd forgiven her for all the lies and deception, but he knew how it felt to be on the receiving end of those lies. And now he'd done the same thing to Stacey. The absolute last person on earth he wanted to hurt.

The worst part was he thought she might already know. He'd seen the look in her eyes as she'd looked at him last night. He wasn't sure what stopped her from saying anything. Maybe she wanted to see if he'd come clean. Or maybe she didn't want to risk waking Rachel, but either way, he had to tell her the truth.

As he pushed his scrambled eggs around on his plate, he watched as she flittered about the kitchen, getting Rachel's bottle ready. Her hair was in that cute, messy ponytail he'd always loved to tug as a kid. She still wore workout shorts from her morning jog…a first since he'd been back in town. He didn't even know she exercised but was glad she had done something for herself. She was giving up far too much for him already.

"Stace?" he asked, not sure how to go about telling her he'd boldly lied to her face.

"Hmm?" she asked, her voice deceptively quiet.

"You know that phone call last night?" He shoveled a mouthful of scrambled eggs to give himself a minute to make sure he got the wording right.

"I recall. The one you said was a wrong number?"

He almost grinned at her sweet tone. He was so busted. And he hoped she'd slap him cross-eyed for it.

"It wasn't a wrong number."

She turned to look at him, her face a mask of neutrality. "It wasn't?"

"No, it was Cameron. A guard let her use his cell phone."

Stacey didn't even blink. "Okay."

Boy, she was going to make him work for it. "I lied to you. And I'm sorry."

She turned and started wiping down the counter. "Why did you feel you needed to lie to me, Joey?"

Wasn't it the million-dollar question? "I don't know. I didn't want to upset you. And it was late."

"And you think by admitting you lied to me now makes it easier somehow?"

"No. I guess I was a little shocked by it all."

"What did she want?"

Joey took a deep breath. "She wants me to bring Rachel to the prison so she can see her."

"And what did you tell her?"

"I told her I'd talk with you."

Stacey spun around, her eyes flashing. "I

might have agreed to act like Rachel's mother, but I'm not. Whatever happens with your little girl is between you and Cameron. I appreciate you telling her you needed to ask me, but in reality, I have no legal right to her. The decision is yours and not ours."

"You're wrong, Stace. Even if we weren't married, I have a feeling I'd be here asking you for advice. You're my best friend."

Crossing her arms, Stacey gave him a motherly look. "Is that all you guys talked about?"

Yup, she definitely had him. "No."

Without a word, she simply watched and waited.

"She asked me if I was happy."

Stacey cocked her eyebrow.

"And if you...pleased me." He grimaced. Did honesty mean full disclosure? "She told me I'd made a big mistake."

When Stacey still refused to say anything, he stood. He ran his fingers through his hair in a frustrated move. "I told her I loved you and I was happy and the mistake was hers, not mine. I was doing the best I could to pick up the pieces."

"How did you feel talking to her?" she finally asked, squinting a little as she evaluated him.

"Honestly, it was a little like old times. I

didn't have enough time to process everything that happened between us before you and I got married. I love you, Stacey, and that's *not* a lie. I think I've loved you since you were a little girl, riding your tricycle all over your yard. But I can't deny Cameron and I had something once. I mean…the proof is sleeping in the other room. But what I wish would go away would be those what-if questions."

Stacey's eyes drifted to the ground, a sure sign he'd said too much. "What if she comes back in eleven months and you divorce me? What then?"

"I'm not going to divorce you. I know my relationship with her was toxic. A marriage would be worse. And on top of everything, Rachel would be in the middle of it all…Stace," he said, bringing her to him. "We work. We fit. We make sense. We're…"

"We're comfortable," she supplied.

"We are," he agreed. "But it doesn't make us wrong. If anything, I think there are a lot of people out there who are married who never achieve what we have. I'd take comfortable over diva any ole day."

She grinned a little. "I guess I just don't understand what you want from me. You say you love me, but Cameron is still with you every day. Where do you see us in a few years?"

Ahhh, a question Joey had tried to avoid

because it meant letting go of the past. A past he didn't really want to be associated with anymore, with the exception of his baby girl, but still found himself drawn like a moth to the flame.

"What do I want from you?" He mulled this question as he watched her pick at some invisible lint on her shirt. She wiggled her toes and waited patiently.

"I want you to love me," he said simply. And he discovered it was true. He wanted Stacey, all of her. Her heart, her soul, the next fifty years.

"I do love you. You know that."

"I want you to love yourself." Her eyes cast downward again, but she didn't hold them there for long.

"I do love myself, Joey. I love who I am when I'm with Rachel."

"What about with me?"

"I'm constantly doubting. Am I saying and doing the wrong things? Should I have worn that instead of this? Will he leave me when Cameron is out of jail?"

Joey felt floored. He knew this was a real fear for her. Even a fear for him, in the beginning. But somewhere over the course of the last few weeks, he'd come to realize Cameron had been merely a phase. A fun and exciting phase, but the excitement had dulled when he'd found out about her lies and deceit. She'd openly admitted she wanted him back once she was out of jail, but Joey had only felt pity for her because she couldn't let go. They would need to work out arrangements for her to see Rachel, but other than that, Joey finally felt the bonds of their relationship lifting.

Slowly, Joey stood. The lump in his throat kept him from saying anything at first. He walked up to her and pulled her into his arms.

"There's nothing I can ever say to you to make you believe I'm not going anywhere. So I'll do the only thing I know to do, Stace."

"What?"

"I'm going to prove it to you. It's going to take me about fifty years, but I hope you'll stick around long enough to know I mean it."

As he pulled back, he saw Stacey's smirk. "I'll hold you to it."

He nodded. "Okay. Deal."

Joey touched his lips to hers for a second. Thinking to be gentle and persuasive, he didn't realize how much his need for this woman grew every time he saw her. He deepened the kiss, and she willingly accepted with a faint moan. She stood on her tiptoes to take all of him in. His hands roamed her back, holding her close and exploring her soft skin under her workout shirt at the same time.

With a gentle shove, Stacey pulled away.

"Rachel needs her bottle."

He watched as she filled the bottle with formula and shook it.

"So what do you think about letting Cameron see Rachel?"

At this, Stacey stopped shaking and her face twisted into something resembling an angry bear. "I don't want my baby getting within a mile of her."

Joey couldn't help the smile. *Her* baby. He liked the sound of that. He wondered if she'd ever be open to having children someday. But now wasn't the time to ask, when she hadn't slept more than three hours intervals in the last few weeks.

"Then she won't. As far as I'm concerned, you're Rachel's mother. No one else. We both have to make those types of decisions together."

"Well, I'm making this one, Joey. I won't have Rachel being confused. I'm the one who loves her enough to sacrifice. Cameron was too selfish, and now she has to deal with her punishment."

Joey watched his wife again. She stood there, shaking the bottle again. Her mouth was set in a determined line and her eyes flashed with fire. She'd never looked more beautiful to him than at that moment, standing up for what she wanted, determined to make it happen.

He nodded. "I couldn't have said it better

myself."

CHAPTER FOURTEEN

THE NEXT SIX months were filled with more of the same. Together, Stacey and Joey had watched Rachel grow and learn. She'd slept through the night by three months old and had sat up by herself by six and a half months. Rachel was babbling, and her toes were her favorite snack.

Joey watched Stacey grow, too. Instead of holding back what she was thinking, she often told him exactly what was on her mind. He loved to see her angry and expressing her opinion. He'd come to realize it wasn't him who held the key to making Stacey more confident, but perhaps it was his daughter.

Cameron still called occasionally in the middle of the night to see how Rachel was doing, and now Joey feared once Cameron was released, she might want visitation and take him to court for it. She'd hinted at this several times, but Joey never waivered from Stacey's wishes. If she didn't want Cameron seeing Rachel, he trusted her instincts and respected her enough to honor them.

When Rachel was four months old, Cameron had called him, demanding again they bring Rachel to the prison the next week. This was Joey's first true fight with Stacey. She'd held a crying Rachel to her breast as if protecting her, shielding her from the world, and Stacey told him in no uncertain terms if he caved and took Rachel to see Cameron, she'd leave him.

At first, he'd been shocked. Then mad. Then proud as punch his wife was standing nose to nose with him, fighting for his daughter's welfare. He'd immediately kissed her and just like that, the fight was over and the subject was dropped.

They had fallen into a comfortable rhythm with each other. Stacey played the housewife part perfectly. Enough that Joey felt guilty she did so much. Sometimes, when she'd had a particularly rough day with Rachel while he was at work, he'd bring home takeout and give her a massage after dinner. Their life was as picture perfect as Joey could have imagined. More so, when he really thought about it.

On weekends, sometimes he gave her money, and she went shopping with his mother. And he couldn't have been more surprised when Stacey came home one day after shopping with a brand new wardrobe, a new, straight hairstyle and missing her glasses. He was happy her cliché duct taped glasses were finally gone, and she now wore contacts. He could gaze into her beautiful green eyes any time he wanted without the light glaring back at him. It was like being married to a different gal now. She'd never been one for fashion, but seeing her in calf-high boots and skinny jeans went a long way to making his mouth water for his wife. Although Joey still preferred her curly hair, the straight was growing on him a little more.

It was during that time he knew things were changing for her…not just outwardly, but inside, too.

It seemed little Stacey Ingram McCrary hadn't needed him after all to make her into a confident, beautiful woman. She handled Rachel with a precision that left him amazed. He didn't think he'd ever be good at changing a diaper or making up a bottle or mixing baby cereal with milk. She could practically do it with her eyes closed. Probably did during the night.

Then there was the bedroom. Over time, Stacey had grown accustomed to his touch, vocalized what she wanted him to do, and left no room for argument when it was bedtime and she was in the mood. She even wore sexy lingerie and blew him away with her svelte curves and wild moves. Her self-confidence was sexier than anything she could wear, and Joey was proud to call her his wife.

It was also during that time, almost seven months after their marriage she experienced her first orgasm. To say he was excited was an understatement, but the look on her face was a memory he would cherish for the rest of his life. It was the kind of bond God had always intended someone to have with their spouse. And he tucked it away, deep inside him so he could recall it during the days to come.

Two days after Rachel turned seven months old, Joey received a phone call at work. His lawyer was letting him know Cameron was up for parole early due to good behavior. A knot twisted in his gut, and nausea threatened to choke him. Everything he and Stacey had worked for in the last seven months was now at stake.

The hearing was set for the following Tuesday. If she was granted parole, she'd then be able to seek visitation rights. The paperwork she'd signed upon entering the prison system would be null and void. His lawyer tried to assure him he'd keep that from happening, but he knew the statistics with mothers and babies. Very few judges felt it was necessary to abolish all contact.

As Joey trudged into the house after work, he wondered how Stacey would take the news. Would she be angry? Retreat back into a shell? Or would she fight for his daughter and her happiness?

But a bigger question flowed into his mind as he entered the front door and looked at Stacey. Her blonde hair flowed around her face as she blew a raspberry at Rachel and then turned those glowing, expressive green eyes toward him and smiled.

Would she give up on them?

STACEY KNEW something was on his mind. Maybe it was his charmingly tousled hair, as if he'd run his fingers through it a million times on the way home, or maybe it was the defeated slouch of his shoulders as he walked through the doors, but she knew something was amiss.

"Bad day?" she asked, hefting Rachel on her hip and walking up to Joey for a kiss.

"You could say that," he muttered, taking off his lightweight jacket. Spring was coming soon, and the days were warmer.

"Wanna talk about it?" she encouraged.

"Yeah, we definitely need to talk about it."

Stacey put Rachel in her high chair and gave her a bottle. "Did you lose your job?"

Joey shrugged. "I wish it was that easy."

She stared at him. His answer meant it could only be one thing. "Cameron."

He nodded and she sat down, thankful the chair was there to catch her.

"Is she out already?"

"Hearing is Tuesday. If it's granted, she can seek visitation."

Suddenly, she was on her feet again. There was no way a drug addict was going to come along and take away her daughter. Stacey wasn't going to let Cameron waltz in and out of Rachel's life and confuse her, either. What kind of mother would either of them be, then?

Stacey had told Joey she'd help him raise his child, and she was going to do just that, in *and* out of the courtroom.

"What about her drug use? If she gets visitation, it has to be supervised. I wouldn't trust her not to get drunk or high and drive off a bridge with Rachel in the car."

Joey's face soured. "Believe me, you're not alone. But we'll need to figure it all out when the time comes. Right now, the lawyer says we have to prepare a testimony on why the judge shouldn't grant her parole."

"I'll get on it as soon as Rachel is down. I can give you fifty reasons why off the top of my head." Stacey came out of her reverie and looked at Joey. His frown tugged at her heart. "We won't let Cameron take her away from us. She's ours."

Joey bit his lip and shook his head. "I love you so much."

A bittersweet smile lifted her lips. "I love you, too, Joe. And I love Rachel just like she came from me. Cameron is toxic, and she won't take our little girl away."

Joey bent at the waist and rubbed his eyes. "I don't even know where to start. If I go after her character, she's going to get ugly. I know her well enough to know that. If I try to play it safe, she'll take advantage. Any good lawyer would."

"Then we'll take the middle road."

"How do we find it?" Joey asked, looking up at her from his seat.

"We have to pray about it. And then we fight."

THE DAY OF the trial came too fast for Joey's peace of mind. Graciously, his mother had offered to keep Rachel while Joey and Stacey attended the hearing. As Cameron was brought into the room in an orange jumpsuit and placed with her lawyer at their table, he wondered what had happened to the girl he'd once loved.

She was so frail looking, and her hair was still cut way too short, even shorter than the day she'd delivered Rachel. One of his favorite pastimes when they were dating had been to brush her long hair. But now, only a couple of inches remained all over her head. She seemed to have aged in the seven months since he'd seen her last. He guessed that's what happened when one dedicated her life to alcohol and drugs.

He glanced at Stacey and her youthful skin and shiny waves. She'd always been the epitome of innocence, but today was an exception. He'd never seen her the way she was right now. Her eyes were trained on Cameron, her back ramrod straight and what he figured was her game face was stoically plastered. She dressed in a blue pinstriped business suit with classic heels. Nothing frilly and no jewelry save the wedding ring he'd given her.

Joey looked down at his ring and smiled. Despite whatever happened today, he still had his baby girl and his wife. He could only pray Cameron wouldn't make him lose the things he held dear.

Cameron turned in her seat and gave Joey a

wan smile. He didn't return her smile. Her eyes darted nervously toward the paper Stacey clenched in her hand. No doubt, she'd figured out they weren't there to support her. In fact, Stacey had a lengthy list of things opposing her parole release. He wasn't sure it would make much of a difference, but at this point, he was desperate.

The judge entered a little while later and a lot of legal jargon went over his head. His lawyer sat on his other side, taking notes and tapping his chin with his pen occasionally.

When the time came for him to speak, Joey finally steeled himself. It wouldn't be easy hurting Cameron. He figured she'd hurt herself enough for both of them, but he was about to unleash some pretty harsh words.

Joey gave his introduction to the judge and looked at Stacey. Her game face hadn't changed, and she watched him without so much of a blink. She was there to support him and it was all that mattered.

"On October 9, 2012, Cameron Matheson called me at approximately one a.m. to ask me to bring my daughter to the prison. She then informed me she was using a prison guard's cell phone. Three more times she called me, once on December 24th, again on January 28th, and lastly on March 18th. Every instance was at approximately one a.m. She said this was to keep the guard out of trouble. When I asked her who this guard was, she wouldn't give me a name, but indicated he let her phone people a lot and also snuck her some drugs in occasionally."

He paused, wiping dampness from his brow and held up his phone records. "I have the phone records and the number highlighted on each of my phone statements here. The officer has since been let go from the Correctional Facility for consorting with a prisoner."

With a quick glance at Cameron, he saw her rounded eyes and her mouth slightly ajar. She probably thought he was playing dirty, but he had another thing to say.

"As for good behavior, I can't say, because I wasn't there. But I know of her behavior prior to conceiving, and I can safely say I don't want my daughter with her out of fear she might relapse and cause an accident. I understand everyone can change, but so far, I've seen little of it, mainly in our conversations with each other at night, and also in my dealings with her before giving birth. Children need their mothers, and I want her to be a mother, but before she can be one to my child, I want her to prove she can be an honest person."

The judge studied him and scribbled something on his notepad. "In your opinion, Mr. McCrary, was Cameron a good person before she turned to drugs and alcohol?"

Joey couldn't help but look at Cameron then. Her eyes were downcast, reminiscent of how Stacey used to look when she didn't believe in herself. But Joey couldn't lie about it. "Yeah, she was. Drugs are a powerful force, and I understand the dependency. That's what I fear the most. Cameron has the potential, but I'm not sure about the willpower. Above all else, I want my daughter to have a happy, loving home surrounded by people who love her. I have no doubt Cameron loves her daughter, but I also have no doubt she has a long way to go before she can provide what a child needs and be a contributing member of society."

"Thank you, Mr. McCrary."

Joey tore his eyes away from Cameron, who now looked at him with tears sparkling in her eyes. It hurt to betray her. He'd once thought she'd be his wife instead of Stacey. She was the woman who had given his baby girl life. He knew how deep the deception could be felt, and the last thing he wanted to do was cause anyone that kind of pain. But he wouldn't go down without a fight when it came to how Rachel would be raised and what she would be exposed to.

That night, Joey lay with his head in Stacey's lap as they talked about the day's proceedings. "I didn't know what else to say. I know she could do it, but I've also seen what a battle it is with drugs. But there's a part of me that says she deserves the chance. Then there's the other part of me that says she gave her chance up when she made the poor choice. At what point do we draw the line, Stace?"

Her cool fingers ran through his hair and circled tenderly at his temples. "There's a lot to think about, and it'll overwhelm us if we let it. But we'll know in a few weeks what the judge's decision is, and we can go from there. Some people can get sober and stay that way, but there's a will there that most people don't have."

"Right. How do we know if she's the exception rather than the rule without risking Rachel's safety?"

"I don't know. I guess the bottom line is, if she's got the willpower, then she'll be willing to do whatever it takes to get her daughter back."

Joey sat up and propped himself up across her lap. "You've changed, Stace. You know?"

She smiled, her bright eyes happy. "I've had a good reason to change."

"It wasn't me. I could have told you how beautiful you were until the cows came home, and you wouldn't have believed me."

"Because I didn't have a reason to believe you. Rachel kind of changed everything with me. When I was the only one she wanted when she was upset, and I spent all those nights with her during feedings, I just realized I have to be the one to give *her* confidence and teach her how to love herself. I can't do it if I don't know how myself. I saw in some way, I was her comfort in a way you and your mother weren't."

"Do you know why?"

Stacey smiled. "Because I'm her mama."

Joey kissed her lips softly. "Exactly. You're her mama. And you're a great mother, Stace. I knew you were amazing, but I don't think the magnitude truly hit me until after I saw how much you loved her and cared about her. Thank you for everything you're doing for her…and for me."

She shrugged. "It's what love is."

"*You're* love. When I think of someone who is a perfect example of love, I always think of you. You've done so much for me, and I've given so little in return."

"You gave me a daughter. And you gave me a husband. Two things I couldn't have had without you."

"You would have had them. I'm just thankful I snatched you up before someone else realized what an amazing person you are."

Stacey smiled.

"I want to have a baby with you, Stace," Joey blurted.

Stacey frowned then laughed. "You do

have a baby with me."

"You know what I mean. I want to make a baby with you. Not now. Not until we're ready for another one, but I've been thinking on it for awhile, and I wasn't sure what you'd think about the idea."

"Hmm…" she said as she unbuttoned the top buttons on his polo shirt and ran her fingertips along his skin. "I think another baby would be stressful right now, but having a baby, especially with you, sounds like a great idea."

"Just think. A little piece of you and me running around with Rachel. How cute would that be?"

Stacey kissed his neck, running her tongue along his hammering pulse. "It would be adorable." Passion filled her gaze, and he wasn't necessarily thinking about a baby just then. But practicing sure was on his mind. There wasn't another woman who could turn him on as quickly or as thoroughly as she did.

"I say let's just practice right now, so when the time comes, we'll have everything down to an art," she whispered. She sucked in his bottom lip between her teeth and nibbled on it.

What could he say to that?

He let out an unintelligible grunt as he claimed possession of her mouth and a little while later, her body.

CHAPTER FIFTEEN

"SHE DOESN'T know you're here, does she?" Cameron asked, squinting as if trying to read a blurry billboard.

"No. I thought it was best I come here alone and talk with you about things," Joey said, feeling the weight of his omission heavily on his shoulders.

"Trouble in paradise?"

"Not at all. I just think we need to settle some things together."

"Like what?"

"Like what's going to happen if you're granted parole and you ask for custody. Is that your intention?"

"She's my daughter. Yes, it's my intention. I haven't seen her since the day she was born, Joe. You won't let me." Her raspy voice filtered through his mind like cotton candy, weaving a convoluted spell on his brain, making him remember things he had no business remembering.

"Do you understand why I've kept her away?" he asked, pushing his thoughts aside.

"Yeah. You're smitten with your new wife and want her to play mommy since I can't."

Her harsh words surprised him since the last time he'd seen her she'd been so accommodating to Stacey. "No, Cameron. I meant what I said in the courtroom. I know you've got it in you to be a good person, and you proved it the day Rachel was born and signed her over to me until you got out. But you understand my hesitancy to bring you into her life when Stacey is all she's ever known."

Cameron leaned back in her chair, studying her nails. "It doesn't change the facts, Joe. I'm her mother. *We* conceived her. You suddenly seem to forget I'm part of the equation here. Prison doesn't mean I stopped existing."

"But it means you made some bad choices."

"Doesn't every one?"

"Yes. But do you even want to do better?"

"I want my daughter. She should be with

me. You're not going to come in here with some psychobabble and make me think I'm not good enough. Rachel might only know your little wife as her mother, but it won't be long before she knows all about me. Do *you* understand, Joe?"

He felt his shoulders slump against his will. "You're missing the point—"

"All I'm hearing is you want more things to throw at me in court when I try to do something to stay in touch with my kid. I'm not giving you any more ammunition. Besides, I know exactly who was behind your little rant in the courtroom."

"Don't blame this on Stacey. She's been there for your *kid* when you couldn't be."

With a sigh, Cameron sat up and took one of Joey's hands in hers. "Joey, I still love you, okay? It hurts me to see you with her. What you said in the courtroom hurt me. And I know she was just a replacement. When I get out of here, I want to try again. We can make it this time. I was terrified of settling down and being stuck with one person the rest of my life who didn't know what went on after dark. But Rachel changed everything for me. I want to share all those new memories with you and be your wife. I know Stacey doesn't please you as much as I did. It's all over your face."

"What doesn't please me is you being a home-wrecker on top of a drug addict. Stacey is the best thing that's ever happened to me, Cameron."

"We both know that's not true," she whispered, looking deep into his eyes.

"Cameron, there's a part of me that will always love you. I could never deny that. That's not a secret. You gave birth to my baby. But getting back together just isn't an option, and I need you to accept it."

Slowly, Cameron nodded. "It still hurts. All this was supposed to be my life and now someone else is living it. You don't sit in a prison cell all day without learning a few lessons."

"I'm sorry. I don't mean to hurt you."

"Then don't hurt me. Let's work together to get me out of here so we can live the life we wanted."

Joey studied her. Since giving birth to Rachel, dark circles were under her blue eyes. He remembered a time when those blue eyes sparkled with mischief and love for him. Now they were dull and lifeless.

"I don't think it's what I want anymore. I just want us to figure out a way to give Rachel the best life possible. I want us to do that together. Without all the lawyers and mud-slinging."

Cameron slowly nodded. "I want that, too."

"Then let's do it."

With great precision, Cameron leaned forward and took his hand in her small one. Her soft skin brought back far too many memories. "On one condition, Joe."

Looking into her eyes, he knew he would do anything to keep things from escalating and jeopardizing his marriage. "What?"

"I want you to come see me every day after work. Until we know if I'm granted parole."

He shouldn't agree. He knew it was just a ploy for her to get under his skin again. His head screamed at him to say no, to tell her it was blackmail, pure and simple. But he thought of Stacey and Rachel at home and how perfect his life seemed the last few months. He didn't want that to go away, and he didn't want Stacey to worry Rachel would be taken from her. If coming here meant keeping peace, he'd do it as long as she wanted.

"I'll be here," he whispered.

"YOU'RE HOME late tonight," Stacey said as she placed a steaming plate of lasagna in front of him. "Rough day?"

Joey thought of his trip to see Cameron and how wounded Stacey would be that he'd agreed to see her every day. But then he thought about how the end justified the means and relaxed a little.

"No, just a lot of things I had to take care of."

She eyed him carefully, but he schooled his expression so he didn't reveal anything. "Like what?"

"Work stuff."

Rachel let out a shriek and they both jumped. With a chuckle, Joey lifted her out of her seat and placed a big kiss on her cheek. "I love you, Itsy Bitsy. How was your day with Mama today?"

Another squeal and her arms flailed. Then she promptly shoved her fingers in her mouth, and a string of drool puddled on her bib. "Mamamamamama."

It was as if time stood still. He lifted his gaze to Stacey's and saw the shock registered on her face. "Did you hear that?" he asked softly.

"Tell me I didn't imagine it," she whispered.

"You didn't. Say it again, Rachel. Ma-ma."

"Mamamamamama," she chanted and reached her arms out to Stacey. Stacey lifted her and spun her around in a circle, then hugged her close, pure joy in her wide eyes and open mouth.

"You said Mama!" she exclaimed and laughed.

"Because you are," he issued, more sure than ever he'd made the right decision with Cameron now.

"I know. What about Da-da? Can you say Da-da?"

"Mamamama!" Rachel squealed again, each syllable getting louder and louder. Then she laid her downy head on Stacey's shoulder and said, "Mamama."

Tears flooded Stacey's eyes, and Joey stood. He wrapped his arms around his family, more excited than ever. Stacey was Rachel's mother, and everything he'd gone through in the last year was suddenly worth it.

"I love you," he said into Stacey's ear. This seemed to make the tears flow faster. He kissed them each away and rubbed his daughter's head.

"I love you, too," she said with a wobbly smile. "And I love you, Rachel."

"Mamama."

They both laughed, and Stacey moved away from him, grabbing Rachel's bottle and feeding her with one hand as she placed her palm on Joey's cheek. The moment intensified when Stacey looked up to him, not a hint of shyness in her demeanor. He barely recognized the woman in front of him anymore. He knew the depth of her transformation went further than he could fathom, but in that moment, he realized he was truly clueless over how much she'd changed.

"Thank you, Joey. Thank you for everything you've given me."

Joey captured her mouth in a quick kiss. "You're thanking me? I'm the lucky one. Always remember that."

A sense of foreboding fell over Joey as they sat down to eat their dinner. He'd make a deal with the devil to protect what was his. But what if he had already done just that?

STACEY WAS starting to worry. Every night for the last week, Joey was late coming home from work. By several hours. As he walked in after nine p.m. eight days later, she simply sent him a look that told him they needed to talk. Rachel was already in bed, and Stacey had some time to think.

"What's wrong?" she asked, wrapping her arms around his shoulders as he sat at the table for dinner.

"Nothing, why?"

"Have I done something to upset you? You haven't been coming home lately until late."

"No, everything's fine. I just have a lot of stuff to do lately."

Placing a kiss underneath his ear, she heard

his harsh exhale and then he dug into his food with fervor.

Still, Stacey couldn't place it, but she knew something was wrong. Joey had been evasive when she asked him questions about his workload, and suddenly it all made sense. Did he not want to be with her anymore? Was there someone else?

She plopped down in the chair and studied him closely. It was as if she wasn't there. Days had passed since they'd last made love or they'd enjoyed a simple night together without any expectations. She knew as soon as he was finished eating, he'd announce he was tired and go to bed.

And she'd follow like a loyal puppy, waiting for a scrap of affection.

The thing was, just as Joey had said, being a mother to Rachel had changed her. It made her see life for what it was now. A fleeting blip on the map God had given her to make a difference in a little girl's life. And possibly the man she'd always loved. But she could only do so much before frustration sat in, and she knew now that was the feeling she had in her chest right then.

She never wanted to go back to being the person she was before Joey came along. That person had been weak and lost and sad from her grandfather's passing. She had direction now. That direction was for Rachel and Joey. Being a wife made her happy, and having someone who came home to her every night felt like warm cookies at Christmastime.

But what if all those fears she thought she'd conquered came racing back? What if, despite all his admissions to the contrary, Joey still loved Cameron and wanted her back? What if, the second she was granted parole, Stacey was served with divorce papers?

He'd made it no secret in the beginning their marriage was no love match. He needed her for Rachel and to help him look stable for the courts. Now that he'd been given temporary custody, did he really need her anymore? Even though the battle wasn't over, he'd put up a respectable fight for his daughter.

If Stacey hadn't already been seated, she might have sat straight on the floor. She worried her lip in an effort to stave off the helpless feeling taking root in her gut. The reality was she couldn't make Joey love her. She couldn't make him stay. And considering he'd been such a player his whole adult life, he'd settled down remarkably fast and furious for a man with so many notches on his bed post. She'd been foolish to let those fears slide by in the name of love.

Now, as he studiously avoided her gaze, she realized Rachel was probably next. She'd be gone, Stacey's life would go right back to where she was when Joey knocked on her door months ago—lonely and scared. Only this time, she wouldn't have her grandfather to help her pick up after the fall.

She missed her grandfather's gentle assurances and his quiet smiles. For all intents and purposes, he'd been both her mother and her father when her parents died. What she wouldn't give for some of his advice.

"I think I'll go to bed," Stacey said and rose on wobbly legs.

He gave her a strange look that spoke of confusion. "I'm not far behind you. I'm exhausted."

"I know you are," she said sadly. It meant there would be no physical affection tonight to keep her fears at bay. The insecurities were rearing their ugly faces again, and she was helpless to stop it. She felt rage consume her. Her hands shook as she grabbed the doorframe, looking back at Joey again.

"Hey, Stace?" he asked without looking up.

"Yeah?"

Finally he turned his expressionless gaze toward her and said, "I love you. You know that, right?"

"Yeah."

But she didn't know anything at all.

JOEY WAS A liar. Plain and simple. Not even just once, but twice now. His visits to see Cameron were eating at him, knowing Stacey waited for him at home and took care of Rachel all so he could stop and feed some strange need Cameron had to see him.

Suddenly his perfect life wasn't so perfect anymore.

He was angry with Cameron for putting him in this position. Even angrier with *himself* for letting her put him in this position. The only good that had come from his visits was how reassured he was doing the right thing. He'd ignored the times his ex entered the visitation room looking pretty and soft, reminding him of the first time they'd met, before the drugs had taken over her life.

He tried to ignore the feelings of doubt he had buried deep inside that told him he was cheating Stacey out of the truth. She would eventually find out what he was doing and she would be angry. Even more hurt. If he got what he deserved, she'd kick him out on his behind.

On the good days, when Cameron said and did everything right, he sometimes wondered what he was doing and how he'd found himself married before he'd worked out all his emotions. Cameron was the first woman he'd loved and wanted to settle down with. Truthfully, the only woman he'd loved and wanted to settle down with. Before he had time to blink, he was married to his friend, and it was a whole new set of feelings he had to deal with. He hadn't loved Stacey in the beginning, and he certainly hadn't wanted a homebody as a wife. He was the fraternity guy at college who hosted parties all the time, for crying out loud!

With Stacey, their love was quiet and assuring, steadfast and powerful. With Cameron, his feelings were wild and wreckless and didn't make a whole lot of sense. Even knowing this didn't stop him from wondering about the what-ifs.

What if she had never started drugs? Would they be somewhere different? Would they still be together? What if he'd worked harder to help her? What if Cameron straightened her life out after prison and never touched drugs again?

He honestly had no idea how he would feel, and it scared him. He liked to think maybe he'd shake off their relationship like water droplets from a shower. And the crazy thing was, if he compared Stacey and Cameron, Stacey always won, hands down. But there was still this pull with Cameron he couldn't put his finger on, and it killed him. He wanted to give everything he had to Stacey, including his heart.

Cameron walked in the visitation room and sat down across from him. She smiled and took his hand in hers. It was something she did every day since he'd agreed to visit her. He let her, mainly because he didn't know how to tell her no.

"I missed you," she said, her eyes bright and alert.

To this, Joey said nothing.

"You seem unhappy. Is everything okay? Is Rachel okay?"

"Everything is fine." Another lie. He was becoming a world-class jerk.

"How is Rachel?" Cameron's eyes went soft and she smiled.

"She's good. She's with Stacey." It was the same comment he gave her every evening.

"Joe?"

He studied their hands, her delicate fingers with blunt nails and his larger ones. He'd once felt they fit together perfectly. "Yeah?"

"I love you. I know you don't want to hear it, but I feel like since you've been visiting, we've been on a different level. Maybe it's because I've been sober for so long, but it's opened my eyes to what a great person you really are. And a great father. Not many men would have done what you did just to save your baby and give up all the fun you had in college to settle down."

"I did what any man should have done. And Rachel isn't a burden to me. She's my daughter, and I love her."

"And I know she loves you. I just wish I was the one you came home to every night."

"You made your choice."

"But it was a stupid one. And we're all entitled to make mistakes, and this was mine."

"What do you want me to say?" He found he was absently rubbing the pad of his thumb across her skin. Suddenly, he pulled his hand away from hers like he'd been burned. What was he doing?

"My lawyer says the judge is looking over my parole tomorrow. We should have an answer by the end of the day."

Panic seized his chest. Did this mean she'd be out of prison and back in his life? Back in Rachel's life?

"What do you think he will decide?"

"I think it will be granted. I'm still doing well here, and I've stopped making those phone calls you tattled on me about. Hard to do when you got the poor man fired." Her smile lessened the sting of her words. "We need to talk about visitation rights with our daughter."

He thought of his selfless wife sitting at home waiting on him, his dinner no doubt hot and ready, his daughter fed and bathed. What right did Cameron have to her? What had she done other than jeopardize her entire existence by her drug use?

Joey looked at her. "What do you suggest?"

"I suggest we split our time with her. She's half mine anyway."

He bit his tongue hard enough to taste blood. "I don't think it makes for much stability in her life being shuffled between us half of the time."

"I gave birth to her, Joe. Don't forget it."

"I haven't. And this isn't about who she belongs to. It's not a personal attack on you. It's about what's good for Rachel and what she needs. And I don't think splitting her life up into fifty percent increments is what's best."

"What do you think is best? For me to fade quietly into the background and let your little wife raise my kid?" Her back was straight and her chin was lifted, a telltale sign she was ready to rumble.

"I think it's best for Rachel to be with the people she knows as her parents. And that's Stacey and me."

"You're delusional if you think I'm going to let her go so easily."

Joey sat up and took her hand in his, hoping against hope he could see the real Cameron when he asked his next question. "Can you honestly tell me you aren't tempted to go back to your old lifestyle?"

"I haven't been out of prison yet, so I can't answer."

"What if you go back to drugs? What if Rachel is with you and you make a big mistake and get behind the wheel of your car with her? How do you think I could live with myself knowing I allowed that?"

It was Cameron's turn to look at their hands. With sad eyes, she shook her head. "I don't know. Maybe we could take it slow. Make sure I'm out of the woods or something. I know it's going to be a temptation."

"So you agree we should do supervised at first? Let Rachel get to know you a little at a time? Make sure you don't relapse before we go full speed?"

Cameron seemed to think a moment. "Yes. I think I could agree to that. I want what's best for her, too, you know. And even though I say it won't happen, I know the reality of my situation. Addiction is addiction."

Sounded like the counseling was working. Or maybe it was what her lawyer had suggested she say so visitation was even an option. Either way, he was on alert and wasn't going to give in to her the way he had for so long.

Abruptly, Joey stood. "I'm glad we agree on something, Cam. I'll be interested to see what happens next."

"Joe!" she said, scrambling from her

position and rounding the table. "I need to know there's hope."

"I told you we'll take things slow with Rachel."

"I mean for you and me. You were the only thing stable in my life, and I need to know we're not over."

"I'm married. What part of those words do you not understand?"

"C'mon, I know that was never a thing for you before. You hit on attached women all the time when you were with me."

"No, I didn't. I was always faithful to you. Always. If there's one good thing I can say for my sordid past, I was always faithful to whoever I dated. I was brought up to believe in marriage as being sacred and irreversible. Stacey and I both feel same way. We were over a long time ago, Cameron, and you need to accept it."

A chilly, stone-like gaze replaced Cameron's pleading one. "It's not smart to go against me right now, Joe. A mother never loses in court."

A moment of dread filled him, but he pushed it back. He wouldn't be intimidated.

"You know coming here to see me puts everything your attorney brings up in question, right?"

And just like that, Joey felt the ball drop. It

was why she'd asked for visits from him. She was planning on manipulating him in court. It all made sense.

"Fool me once, shame on you. Fool me twice…" he said sadly, shaking his head at his own stupidity.

"That's just it, Joe. You've always been an easy target. I don't like what I've had to do to get visitation, but I'm determined to spend time with my daughter. No matter what."

Without a word, Joey backed up. The lump in his throat was more than he could take. He didn't want her to see him break down and cry like a baby.

Now everything he held dear, his wife, his daughter and his own sanity was at risk because of one prisoner. He didn't know what ever possessed him to love Cameron so deeply.

"Joe," she said, her voice soft. "I didn't want to hurt you…"

He held his hands up to silence her as he continued to the door.

"I still love you, Joe. Even if you don't believe me. But it's like you said, being a parent changed me. And I deserve to know my little girl."

I, I, I, was all Joey heard. What about Rachel? Last time he checked, it wasn't about him or Cameron, but about what stability Rachel should have.

Without a backward glance, Joey left the prison and told himself he wasn't going to return. Whatever feelings he thought he'd felt for Cameron blew away like sand in a storm. And what a storm it was.

CHAPTER SIXTEEN

THE MOMENT Joey walked in that night, Stacey knew something was truly wrong. Anger was all over his face, more pronounced in his clenched jaw and furrowed brows.

"Is Rachel asleep?" he asked without a greeting, throwing his briefcase on the table.

"Y-yes," Stacey said and took his plate out of the microwave.

"No. I can't eat right now. We need to talk."

Stacey slowly closed the microwave door, giving herself time to regroup. "Have I done something?"

"Stace, there's nothing you could ever do to

upset me like this." He came up behind her and kissed her hair, his masculine scent surrounding her and making her feel cozy despite the seriousness of his situation.

"Let's go sit in the living room. This might take awhile."

Again, Stacey took her time following Joey into the living room. She wasn't sure what was about to happen. Would he tell her tonight he was having an affair? Wanted a divorce? Needed space?

"I need to tell you something," he said, running his hands down his face.

With a deep breath and a thick swallow, she nodded. "Okay."

It took Joey a minute to spit out the words and when he did, she was floored. "I've been going to the prison to see Cameron."

The betrayal sank deep inside Stacey. Maybe it would have been easier with someone who didn't have such a history, or easier because another woman was prettier or skinnier, but Cameron was the very woman who had given her a husband and a child. In a weird sort of way, she owed everything she had to her. But just as she'd always known in the back of her mind, her happiness was only temporary. She wasn't cut out for a man like Joey. People like him wanted it all. They wanted the trophy wife and the flashy cars, not a childhood friend for a wife who drove a used vehicle.

"I think you should pack your things," she said softly. Ironically, tears didn't come. Just a sad acceptance.

"Stacey, let me explain."

"You lied to me. Again. I asked you not to."

"I was trying to protect what we have! She said if I came to see her, she'd work with me on visitation rights. I thought it would be easier on all of us!"

It was too much. Stacey shook her head and stood. "I can't trust you. I'm not sure I ever have now."

"Don't do this."

"You did it, not me. I got dragged into this and had stars in my eyes, Joey! I thought somehow you'd fall in love with me, and we'd live happily ever after. I wasn't *thinking*!" Furious with herself now, she threw a pair of socks at him, not even stopping to consider how silly it was.

He caught them easily and stared at her.

"Get out."

"I promised you I wouldn't leave you. I don't want this to be over." His eyes shone bright, and Stacey felt the anger boiling to a full roll.

"Don't men like you make promises just to prove you can break them? Then you call up all your friends and laugh about it?"

"I wouldn't do that to you."

"No, but you'd sneak around behind my back and see your ex girlfriend who is in *prison*! I'm not sure what's worse, you lying to me or that I'm not any better than a drug-addicted convict."

Stacey tried to avoid him, but he backed her into the same corner of the living room where they'd shared their very first adult kiss.

"I did it because I thought she would make it easier on us to keep our family together."

"You're a fool for her, Joey. And I'm a fool for thinking anything would be different. I need some space. I can't sleep next to you tonight knowing you've lied to me and taken away my faith in you."

"I'm not leaving you. I don't care how mad you are at me. We're going to work through this. I promised you I wouldn't leave you, and I'm going to prove to you I won't. If I don't do anything else right, I hope I can manage this."

"Suit yourself."

"Tomorrow is the hearing for Cameron's parole. I don't expect you to come, but I have to be there by eight. She's expecting to walk out of there afterward."

Stacey turned and looked at him, sadness emanating throughout her body. "Maybe you guys can have your happily ever after after all.

Count me out."

Without warning, Joey pinned her against the wall, his hands gating her in with no chance of escape. "You're my *wife*, Stacey. I need you there. No one has ever been there for me like you have. What am I going to do when the judge sees you're not there? How do you think it will effect visitation? If you don't do it for me, do it for Rachel. She deserves being with someone she knows. Not a stranger who could kill her if she makes a bad decision."

Numbness made her next words come out colder than she ever wanted to be about the little girl she'd come to love as her own. "You made the choice to lie to me. You made the choice to do something without consulting me. Rachel is an innocent bystander in all this, and I'm really sad you've made the wrong decisions so far in your life. But you've made your bed, and now you have to sleep in it."

The soft thud of the door closing behind her as she entered their bedroom was like a gunshot echoing through the night. Or maybe it was the dam that held back her tears crumbling into dust.

THE NEXT MORNING, it was clear Joey hadn't slept well. Stacey hadn't either, but she'd refused to help him when Rachel cried during the night. Despite the urgent calls she kept hearing. "Mamamamama!" She refused to go to her. It was best to make the transition a clean one. They were both way too attached, it seemed.

As she entered the kitchen, she didn't even bother to look their way, but from her peripheral vision she saw Joey was feeding Rachel baby food, and Rachel was pouting and shoving the food away.

"You've got to eat, baby," he cooed, spooning another bite toward her. Stacey looked and saw he was trying to feed her peas. She hated peas, and if he wasn't careful, she'd throw up on him. The only thing that stopped her from letting him figure it out on his own was knowing how uncomfortable Rachel would be getting sick.

"She hates peas," she stated simply and handed him a jar of applesauce. "Especially for breakfast."

Joey looked relieved and gave her a weak smile. "Good to know. Listen, Stace…"

She held up her hand, effectively silencing him. "That wasn't an invitation to speak to me. The more I think about this, the angrier I get. The only reason I'm speaking to you is because of Rachel."

A few moments of silence reigned

peacefully as Rachel ate and Joey spooned. She fixed herself some fruit for breakfast and kept her back to Joey. She was a marshmallow when it came to him, and if she wasn't careful, she'd be right back where she started, shy, embarrassed, and willing to do anything for him, no matter what the cost to her own heart.

Heat surrounded her as Joey's hands urged her to turn around.

"No," she issued.

"Yes. We need to talk." His hands were insistent, but she held on to the counter.

"You're not going to make me any less angry by trying to sweet talk your way out of this. You hurt me, Joey."

"Will you look at me?"

"No."

"Please?"

Slowly, she turned. It wasn't smart but then again, she'd never made good grades in school.

"I'm sorry I made you cry," he said softly. "It was all I could do not to take down the door and hold you. The only thing stopping me was knowing it might hurt you even more."

Stacey kept her gaze trained on a piece of lint on his shirt. Sometimes saying nothing at all was easiest.

"I'm sorry I lied to you. I promise you I never intended to hurt you or make you feel like less than the wonderful wife and friend you are to me. I knew in my heart it was wrong the whole time, but I reasoned the end would justify the means. If I could get Cameron to back down on visitation, maybe I could live with my choice."

Again, she said nothing. Everything he said was an excuse. A justification of what he'd done to cut her so deeply.

"What else do you want me to say?" he asked after a moment of her silence.

"I shouldn't have to tell you what to apologize for, Joey."

"I don't want you to, but I am curious if there's anything else I've done that maybe I haven't realized. I am a man, you know."

"How about loving Cameron more than me?"

"Do you really believe that?" He pulled back and looked in her eyes. Stacey met his gaze square on, showing him how serious she was.

"Do you feel like you should apologize for it, Joey? For loving another woman more than your wife?"

"But I haven't! I don't!"

"No? Every choice you've made has been for her." She moved away from him, his heat leaving her cold in its wake. "I can't live like this. I fooled myself into thinking I could love you enough for the both of us. But it was just a simpleton's dream. You and I both know this won't work until you've settled your feelings with Cameron."

"But I have, Stacey! These visits with her proved to me what I knew all along!"

Stacey shook her head. "No, they didn't. The fact you can't see that tells me everything I need to know."

"What do you want from me?"

Stacey startled a little at his raised voice, but she squared her shoulders and cocked an eyebrow at him. "I want you to love me."

"I do love you! I've told you a million times!"

"I don't want a feeling, Joey. Love isn't always mushy smiles and hugs and kisses. Those things fade with time. It's gritty. It's hard. And it's a choice."

"What are you talking about?"

Why did it surprise her so that he didn't understand? Back when her faith was stronger, before her duties as a wife had caused her to slip with her daily Bible readings, she'd loved one particular passage. It gave her hope one day she'd find the kind of love Jesus spoke of in regard to her husband:

"Love is patient, love is kind. It does not envy, it does not boast, it is not proud. It is not rude, it is not self-seeking, it is not easily angered, it keeps no record of wrongs. Love does not delight in evil but rejoices with the truth. It always protects, always

trusts, always hopes, always perseveres."

Could she say she was being the kind of spouse he wanted? Certainly she was justified in being angry at his lies about Cameron. And she was right to feel betrayed. But that didn't mean she could negate their marriage on a lie. Marrying him was her choice, right or wrong. She wasn't perfect either.

But she wasn't ready to admit anything to him yet. And now was as good a time as any to demonstrate what she wanted from him.

"If you'll give me ten minutes, I'll get ready to go to the courthouse with you."

"You're going?"

She looked at him with a frown. "You said you needed me to go, didn't you?"

He swallowed so hard she saw his Adam's apple bob with the effort. "I do need you."

"Ten minutes."

And she walked into the bathroom, a prayer on her lips.

CHAPTER SEVENTEEN

THE COURTROOM was cold and sterile, much like Stacey found the hospital room to be where Rachel had been born. Cameron still hadn't come in yet, and Joey sat next to her bouncing his leg so fast she was getting annoyed.

Rachel squirmed in her arms, and she fought to keep her happy.

"I think I'll take her outside. She's getting restless," Stacey said, feeling a bit overwhelmed. They went out to dinner sometimes with Rachel, but it had never been necessary to keep her quiet.

"I'll take her," Ms. McCrary said behind her in a hushed whisper. Stacey hadn't been sure if her mother-in-law could come, but she was glad she had. It was nice to have a friendly face there.

When Rachel was out of the courtroom, Joey gently took Stacey's hand and kissed her fingertips. "Thank you for coming, Stace. It means the world to me."

"I did what any decent wife should do."

"Maybe so, but it doesn't mean I appreciate it any less."

Stacey nodded silently and squeezed his hand. "It's what love is, Joey. And I've meant it every time I've said I love you."

Only for her, the feelings also came with the choice.

Joey didn't say anything and before long, Cameron was ushered in. Her blue eyes honed in on Joey immediately, looking sad and a bit lost. Then, her gaze landed squarely on Stacey's.

At first, Stacey wasn't sure what to do. She almost pulled her grip away from Joey, but he tightened his hold and she sensed he needed her touch then. Whether it was a touch he wanted from a friend or his wife, she might never know, but she did know she couldn't deny him.

Cameron offered her a wan smile, void of any emotions and sat down, keeping her back to them.

Joey rubbed his fingers across the back of her hands. When she looked at him, she saw his gaze was centered across the room, at nothing in particular. What was he thinking? What she wouldn't give to know right then.

"Mamamamama!" Rachel's voice called out just before the hearing was about to start.

Stacey turned and smiled as Ms. McCrary brought Rachel in. The second she took her baby girl, it hit her like a punch to the gut. Cameron had just witnessed everything. And not only that, the first time she'd seen her daughter since the day she was born, she was calling another woman her mother. Stacey's heart hurt *for* her. But she didn't feel guilty.

Turning slowly, she saw Cameron watching them with huge tears in her eyes. Not knowing what to do, she sat down next to Joey again. Rachel laid her head on her chest and shoved her thumb in her mouth. Stacey wasn't up to speed on how she should behave, so she decided not to act any different with Rachel than she had since day one. She wanted Cameron to see Rachel was in good hands.

Stacey just didn't want Cameron to think she'd been replaced, even if Rachel didn't know the difference.

As the judge came in and the hearing started, Stacey frowned at Cameron, huddled with her lawyer. Something in her gut told her it wasn't good, especially when they both turned and looked at her holding Rachel.

She and Joey exchanged looks, but eventually he shrugged and turned his attention to the judge.

They soon learned Cameron's parole had been granted, and she would be released from prison immediately. The judge then set the custody hearing for the following week. Until then, she wasn't allowed to see Rachel.

It all happened so fast, Stacey wasn't sure what to make of it. She did have enough presence of mind to realize they had one week to make sure Cameron couldn't hurt Rachel. One week. After so many months with the baby she'd come to know as her daughter, it came down to the next seven days to prepare her for an introduction to her biological mother.

When Stacey was honest with herself, there was no way a judge wouldn't grant some sort of visitation for Cameron. And even worse, she wasn't sure what would be best for her little girl. Should she know the woman who gave birth to her? Stacey needed to think on all this and pray. God would give her the peace of mind she needed to get through the next few days and coming months.

"Well, I guess that's that," Joey said, standing and watching Cameron exit the room. She didn't even look back as the door clicked behind her.

"A week, Joey. In one week, it'll be over,

and we can quit wondering. We'll have answers then. And we can learn how to deal with them."

Despite the fact she felt worlds apart from her husband since he'd revealed his lies, she still leaned into him when he wrapped his arms around her. "We'll deal with it together, no matter what, Stace. I love you."

Stacey's world crumbled all over again.

WOULD STACEY leave him? Joey wanted to believe she wouldn't. Needed to believe she wouldn't. But when push came to shove, he just didn't know what their outcome would be once Cameron was in their lives again. She'd always been the pink elephant in the room with them, but he was determined to make the next seven days the best he'd spent with his family yet.

"Let's go away together, Stace," he said the next evening. "Just you, me and Rachel. Let's go to the beach and spend our days playing in the sand and eating seafood. I want us to be together as a family."

"We've been together as a family for a while now, Joey," she said as she folded a onesie.

"I know. But I also know we're both feeling the pressure of next week's custody hearing. We need a few days away."

"I'm game for anything you'd like to do," she said with a small smile.

He still didn't feel like they were back on even ground. It was all his fault, like he hadn't apologized enough or done enough to make her understand how much he regretted his bad decisions. And not only had he made poor decisions, they'd also had very little time together as a couple since they'd gotten married. After all, Rachel had been born only a few days after they'd said their I do's.

"I've made reservations for us. Will you come with me?" He stood and walked over to her, taking the onesie and putting it in the right pile.

"Yes."

"Look at me, Stace."

She did as he commanded but said nothing.

"I love you so much. You've done a lot for Rachel and me. You're the most amazing person I've ever known."

"There were some selfish motivators in there, too. I got to have the family I've always wanted."

"Either way, there's very little I could do to ever repay you."

Stacey studied his chest for a moment and then smiled. "I don't want you to repay me. Just love me."

With a smile, Joey kissed her nose. "I do."

"Love me even when things get tough."

"I will."

"Love me enough to always tell me the truth."

"Deal."

Joey took her face in his palms and ran his thumb along her cheekbone. His wife was the most beautiful woman to him. Not just physically, although there was plenty of physical attraction, but her beautiful heart was enough to challenge Mother Teresa for Woman of the Year. He wasn't sure when it had happened, but he'd come to discover he needed Stacey in a way he'd never needed Cameron, or his mother, or any of his friends.

Stacey balanced him in a way he couldn't describe. She gave his life purpose and made him want to be a better person. Along the way somehow he'd screwed up and hurt her deeply, but through it all, his heart had never waivered. She was the woman he wanted to be with.

Slowly, giving her time to pull away, he lowered his mouth to hers and claimed her lips in a kiss meant to show her how much he truly loved her. Their lovemaking had never been wild or reckless, but this kiss surpassed anything they'd ever experienced together.

Finally, they were getting somewhere.

CHAPTER EIGHTEEN

THE COOL SPRING evening brought back memories of Stacey's childhood with Joey and the evenings they spent together in their early teens. She remembered on nights like this how they'd sat behind his parent's barn and talked about anything and everything. One night stood out in particular.

"What do you want in a wife one day, Joey?" she'd asked him, hoping against hope she might be the one to win his heart.

"I want her to be beautiful. To love life. To be the only man that'll ever be in her life. Big boobs. Those are a must."

Stacey grinned as the balcony door slid

open and Joey's arms came around her. He pressed a soft kiss against her temple. His fingers brushed her hair to the other side despite the ocean breeze.

"I'm glad we got away for a few days," Joey mumbled, placing hot, open-mouth kisses on her neck.

She didn't realize she'd groaned out loud until Joey chuckled in her ear. "I'll never get enough of you."

"I hope not," she whispered. She let Joey have his way with her right there on the balcony, overlooking the Gulf of Mexico. Afterward, he settled her in his lap and ran his hands up and down her arms, warding away the chill.

"There's something about you lately..." he began, seeming to need a moment to think of what he was trying to put a finger on.

She stayed quiet and waited. He didn't disappoint.

"You've changed since we got married. Even more than I realized, I think."

Stacey smiled against his warm chest. "I know what I want in life now."

"Tell me."

The arrogance that was so Joey filled his words, and she remembered a time when it was as much of a turn on as it was a turn off. Now she didn't mind it a bit.

"I want you. I want Rachel. I want our family."

Joey squeezed her closer and exhaled. "When Rachel's a little older…maybe in six months or a year or so…I want to have a baby with you."

Stunned, Stacey sat straight up and looked into his eyes. It was dark on the coast, but she could still see his expression. Gone was the arrogance and now uncertainty filled his gaze.

"Are you sure? It means you'd be tied to me forever."

"Aren't we already?" His fingertips trailed her jaw and traced her lips as she watched him.

"I mean if you decide …"

"What's it gonna take to make you understand I'm not going anywhere? I'm not going to decide to leave you. I love you."

And there were those words again. The words she had no doubt he meant, but it was clear he didn't understand. She kept hoping and praying she would be able to be the example of love to him to realize even when things weren't perfect, she'd still be there. He was still hanging on to the newness of their relationship, the *feeling*. But what about when those feelings went away? It was inevitable that they would.

"Will you still love me if I gain eighty pounds when I'm pregnant?"

His smile was brilliant against the night. "I

think I'd love you even more because it would be my baby inside you."

"And when I get cranky and you can't live with me anymore?"

"I'll build a house next door."

With a giggle, she slapped his arm playfully and settled her head on his chest again, listening to his strong and steady heartbeat.

"I mean it, Stace. I said I do, and I meant it. I want us to move past whatever this is between us and live our lives together."

Stacey exhaled. "Lying to your wife is a pretty big deal, Joey. I'm still processing. I forgive you, but I still need time to process."

"If you forgive me, what's left to process?"

"The hurt. The anger. Convincing myself you didn't do it to hurt me."

"You know I wouldn't hurt you on purpose!" He sat upright, taking her by the shoulders and looking her directly in the eye.

"Logically, no you wouldn't. But I *am* female. I tend to be a little irrational sometimes."

"I wish I could say if I could take it all back, I would. But I learned something important during those visits with Cameron."

Again, Stacey waited for his epiphany.

"I never really loved her. Well, maybe in some small way I did, but the connection I had with her wasn't what I thought it was. Mostly just a firewall to keep me off the trail of secrets. Just an illusion."

"And that makes you sad." Stacey could hear in his voice. He couldn't deny it.

"Yeah, it does. And I'm sorry if it hurts you, but I don't think anyone goes into a relationship with someone expecting it to end. And we conceived Rachel. I certainly didn't expect it to end the way it did."

"Do you wish things were different?"

"In some ways, sure. But all the ways I do are superficial and part of an illusion she created. Do I wish things were different with us? Absolutely. Only because I wish I could go back and start with you and never been in this whole mess to begin with."

"It's gonna get a lot harder before it gets better."

"I know. Cameron won't give up custody and she'll fight just to see me lose."

"But I'll be here the whole time, Joey. Even if a judge decides Cameron should have her all the time, I'll be here to pick up the pieces. And we'll make the best of the situation we have."

Slowly, Joey's hands slid down her arms and he took her hands in his, looking out to the rolling ocean. The only thing they could see was the white foam of each new wave hitting the shore.

"Would you have married me if Rachel hadn't been part of the bargain?"

Stacey grinned. "Probably not."

Joey's gaze darted to hers.

She laughed. "I would have married you if all you had to offer me was a cardboard box and an overpass. Rachel was just a bonus."

"You're a great mom. A great wife. It doesn't get better than you. I'll spend the rest of my life making it up to you for my mistakes with Cameron."

Stacey closed her eyes and brought her forehead to his. "We both have a lot of insecurities about this marriage," she said with a sigh. "But we'll work it out. If nothing else, we're friends. And friends is more than most people have."

"Agreed."

"Let's take Rachel down to the beach tomorrow and build a sandcastle. Go get some seafood by the dock. What do you say?"

"I think it sounds perfect."

"You know what else sounds perfect?" Joey asked. He stood and brought her with him.

"What?"

"Holding you all night and waking up to you in the morning."

"You're a sap."

"Guilty as charged."

They slipped back into the room where

Rachel was quietly sleeping in her crib and crawled into bed together. Despite the lies and all turmoil their eight month marriage had been through, one thing was clear as Joey fit his body against her back and looped his arm around her.

They fit together perfectly.

"NO NO! RACHEL! You don't eat the sand!" Stacey explained as she tried to stop the chubby fist from succeeding in its venture.

Joey laughed at the sight even as his heart warmed. Maybe he had turned into a sap, but he had a good reason. Who wouldn't sap away with a beautiful wife and a kid so cute he couldn't stand it? He was a blessed man, and he never wanted to forget it.

"Rachel!" Joey called, trying to get his daughter's attention before more sand became the object of her attention. "Look! Let's build a sandcastle!"

Her yellow bonnet blew in the ocean breeze, lifting at its ends. Her blue eyes looked up at him as she patted the bucket he overturned.

"Yes, baby girl, pat the bucket! We'll get the sand out and build a castle for Daddy's princess."

When he lifted the bucket, the sand held its

shape…for all of five seconds. Before he knew it, Rachel had dived in, destroying his eighth attempt to build a castle.

Maybe she was a bit young for this kind of escapade? Across from him, Stacey sat in her shorts and tank top, muffling her laugh.

"Go ahead. Get it out."

Stacey threw her head back and laughed a loud, joyful laugh. "She's impossible."

"She's eight months old," he said, feeling the need to defend her.

"And you're an amazing daddy. Pretty determined, too. I would have given up seven buckets ago." Rachel let out an ear-piercing squeal and clapped her hands together. Joey flinched but scooped her up and planted a kiss on her sandy cheek.

"Love you, baby girl," he said. She promptly put a soggy, sandy hand on his cheek and smeared it across his skin. Then she leaned forward with open lips and gave him her typical baby kiss.

His heart melted. He'd build her a thousand sand castles to knock down if it was what she wanted.

The click of Stacey's phone warned him he had been captured.

"I think I'll frame this one."

Joey put Rachel down and crawled over to Stacey and puckered his lips. She gave him a small peck and grinned. "What?"

"I love watching you with her."

"Ditto. Guess we're both pretty smitten with each other, huh?"

Stacey gave him a careless shrug. "Most days."

"What happened to the cardboard box we could live in?"

"I just meant it would be less for me to clean up when you came home from work."

"Oh yeah? I think you'll pay for that!"

He tackled his wife on the sand and tickled her. Stacey's loud guffaws caused him to laugh and before he knew it, Rachel was squealing and laughing with them.

After a thorough kiss, Joey pulled Stacey up and helped her brush the sand out of her hair. "It's been a perfect day, Ms. McCrary. This vacation was just what we needed."

For a moment, they simply stared at each other. Joey didn't know what she was thinking, but he was grateful for every moment the three of them had together. He'd watched Rachel grow for eight months now, seen many of her firsts, and with all that threatened, he wanted to hold on even tighter.

"Love you," he whispered.

"Love you, too," she whispered back.

Her gaze snapped to Rachel just as his did. A big fistful of sand was headed straight for her mouth.

"NO!" they exclaimed in unison, diving toward her hand.

CHAPTER NINETEEN

The night before the custody hearing, Joey couldn't sleep. Stacey breathed heavily next to him. She wasn't having the trouble he was. He hadn't heard a peep out of Rachel, either, but her nights of waking every four hours were long past.

The vacation they'd taken together was certainly needed, but the second they'd arrived home, it was like there was a giant elephant in the room again. He wished he knew how to make Stacey trust him again, or at least talk things out with her. But she remained steadfast there was nothing for them to talk about. She forgave him.

But it wasn't. She still needed something from him, but he didn't have a clue what it could be. He'd already told her he would never leave her, and short of chaining himself to the house, he didn't know what else to do to make her understand his heart was with her.

He'd admitted he wanted children with her. It was a fact. To see her round with his baby inside her, all glowing and happy...Joey sighed at the thought. He loved being a father and loved Stacey being his children's mother.

He'd confessed his love over and over again. He didn't have a whole lot to compare his feelings to, mainly because he'd never felt this way. Stacey was his friend, his lover, the mother of his child. They'd been intimate long before he knew what he felt for her was love, but he'd also loved her faith in God and how she prayed at night. He loved how she looked at him like he hung the moon. And he loved the person she brought out in him. A man who wanted to shuck off the old and welcome the new life he was foraging for them.

He didn't think his love for her could go any deeper, but still she wasn't one hundred percent happy. He saw it in the expectant, hopeful gaze as he told her how much he loved her every day. But he always fell short if her looks of disappointment at the end of the day were indicators.

Maybe he was destined to be punished for his actions thus far. But he found it hard to believe anyone, let alone God, could punish Stacey for *his* actions. No, he would figure it out. He would make her completely happy and wouldn't stop until those expectations were met. Whatever they were.

Then there was the matter of his daughter. He hadn't prayed in a long time, but it was time to get on his knees and pray the judge would deem him the appropriate parent. Even if he did, he knew Cameron could try for custody again down the road, but to know he had more time to show his baby girl how much he loved her and cared for her, he'd be able to at least relax some.

So Joey did what he hadn't done in a long time. He prayed. He asked God to forgive him for all of his sins, to forgive him for hurting Stacey, to forgive him for giving Rachel a poor start to life. Joey sank to his knees, asking God for the judge to see he was a good father, trying to make the best of a bad situation and do right by his flesh and blood. And he prayed God would look into his heart and know Rachel was his joy, a true blessing no matter the circumstances with which she came to him.

When he was done, he felt immensely better. Stacey had certainly taught him to rely on God during the tough times, but she'd also shown him to stand up for what he believed. And tomorrow, in the courtroom, he'd fight tooth and nail for his little girl. The judge wouldn't know what hit him.

STACEY WATCHED Cameron walk into the courtroom. Funny how different she looked when she wasn't in prison orange. Instead, she wore a black pencil skirt and a silk blouse. Very professional. Her hair was pulled back in a low bun and glasses were perched on her nose. She looked ready to play the part of doting mother.

Stacey adjusted a sleeping Rachel in her arms and glanced at Joey. He was staring straight ahead, a sheen of sweat visible on his brow.

"No matter what, Joey, we'll be fine. And so will Rachel."

"We both know that's a lie."

His abrupt demeanor brought her up short. Perhaps it was better to keep quiet until the verdict was read.

A little while later, Joey went to sit with their lawyer and the judge entered to begin the proceedings. The defense presented their argument to the judge. Cameron had been drug-free during her prison sentence and remained so since her exit from jail. Cameron had been a model prisoner—whatever that was—and had proven she could be trusted.

Then came the hard part. They began attacking Joey's character. It was all she could do not to stand up and shake her finger at Cameron.

"Mr. McCrary spent many evenings at the State Prison with the defendant here, at her request. He never once told his wife and left her to take care of the infant Ms. Matheson bore. Until the day of her release from prison, Ms. Matheson hadn't seen her daughter, or even held her since the day she was born. Eight months is a long time for a mother not to be with her child. I ask for Your Honor to consider these facts and grant Ms. Matheson sole custody of her daughter."

It was all Stacey could do not to cry as she sat there holding Rachel. Her sweet, chubby body was so relaxed, so trusting that tears threatened to burst from her eyes. *She* was Rachel's mother. Not Cameron.

"At this time, I'll give Mr. McCrary a chance to voice his objections to Ms. Matheson's custody request," the judge said with a nod toward Joey. Slowly, Joey stood and straightened his dress coat, buttoning it as he walked to the podium. She knew him well enough to know he was taking his time to gather his emotions and his thoughts.

With a deep breath, he began. "I'd like to stand here and say that Cameron would be a horrible mother. Or maybe even say she has no right to be a mother. But the truth is, I can't tell you anything because I don't know her. I don't know Cameron Matheson at all.

"Cameron Matheson asked me a few months ago to come to the prison to visit her so we could talk about custody for my daughter. I was happy to oblige and hoped we could work something out for supervised visitation. Even so, I hesitated. What if she used drugs again and Rachel was with her? What if she couldn't say no and drove with my helpless baby in the car with her?

Joey shook his head and frowned down at his paperwork.

What was he thinking? Stacey wondered. She held her breath.

"IT ALL COMES down to choice," Joey finally said to the judge. In that moment, everything had come together like one of the last pieces of a puzzle sliding perfectly into place.

"We all have a choice to make. I'll be the first to admit I've made some bad choices in my life, but I've also made some really good ones." Joey glanced back at his wife with his sleeping baby in her arms and smiled. His relationship with Stacey had begun with a choice, too. To do right by his daughter or let her go into foster care.

"I wasn't ready to be a father, but I wanted what was best for Rachel. I chose to give up late nights and not taking life too seriously. I chose to be my little girl's father. And I'm good at it.

"I chose to marry a woman who is not only my best friend, but a wife I *never* have to worry about misleading me in any way. And she has taken care of my daughter as if she'd given her life from her own body. She's the only mother Rachel knows because of Cameron's choices. Her bad choices.

"I'm not saying Cameron can't change. I'm not saying she'll be a user forever, but I'm asking for the opportunity to make sure she doesn't slip into those bad habits again. I ask for supervised visitation until our next hearing and periodic drug tests." He turned to Cameron and heaved a sigh.

"I'm asking you to make a choice, Cameron. I'm asking you to love her more than you love yourself. To put aside any hatred between us so we can do what's right by her. This has nothing to do with you and me, and everything to do with what's best. That's all I want."

With a solemn nod to Cameron and then

the judge, Joey took a seat. It was a waiting game now. Joey was happy with what he'd said, and it was all in the hands of the judge now. Not just the judge's hands, but God's.

A ten-minute recess was called, and Joey sprang out of his chair and rushed to Stacey. She took his hand in hers and smiled wanly. "Your speech was perfect."

He looked at her. Another piece of the puzzle took shape. "When we're done here, we need to talk."

Stacey's eyes went round. She took a deep breath.

"I think you'll be happy with what I have to say."

"One thing at a time, Joey."

He bent to kiss her.

"Joe?" he heard behind him. Cameron.

Joey turned and met Cameron's sorrowful gaze. "I've had some time to think."

Joey stood there, not sure what to do.

"And what you said…it's true. I've made some really bad choices, like blackmailing you to come see me at the prison. I'm really sorry for that, and I'm sorry, Stacey, for any trouble it caused the two of you. He never waivered in how much he loved you." She took a deep breath and smiled bravely. "But I like to think I can still do what's right by her though. So I'm gonna make a choice." Cameron's face screwed up and tears fell down her cheeks. "I'm gonna choose to take myself out of the equation. Stacey, you're all she's ever known as a mother, and she loves you. She sees you as her mother. I'll never forgive myself for not making the choices I should have made long before she was ever conceived. I'm choosing to give her to you, Joe. Maybe when she's older and can protect herself a little more, we can talk again, but right now, I can't interfere."

Joey swallowed down the lump at seeing Cameron this way. She was suddenly the woman he'd known all those years ago. "You're making the right choice. And I'm more than happy to talk about things later on."

When Cameron didn't leave, Joey felt the need to do more than just stare. "Come here," he whispered, and gathered her into his arms. She went willingly, crying the whole way. "She'll be just fine. And happy as a clam," he reassured her.

"Without me. That's what hurts so much," she mumbled into his jacket.

Joey risked a glance back at Stacey and saw Stacey was holding Cameron's hand and squeezing it. Just as Joey let her go, he realized Rachel was awake.

Cameron lifted hopeful eyes to him. "Can I hold her? Say goodbye?"

He nodded solemnly. What else could he

do? The woman was willingly giving up the fight.

Slowly, Stacey placed Rachel in Cameron's arms. Her tears returned full force. "Oh, baby," she cried. "You're so beautiful. The absolute best part of your daddy and me. I'll never forget you, and I'll never stop trying to be a better person so we can have a relationship when the time comes. For now, you grow up happy and healthy and know you've got two mommies who love you more than life itself."

Joey cleared his throat to rid himself of the lump forming in his throat. Stacey's eyes were bright with unshed tears. The scene was touching, knowing Stacey's heart ached for the woman despite everything.

Cameron gave Rachel back to Stacey. "Go back to Mama," she whispered. "I love you."

Without another word, she turned and walked back to the table with her lawyer, entering into a deep discussion. Joey could tell the lawyer didn't like Cameron's backpedaling, but after a solemn nod, the lawyer stood and exited the courtroom toward the judge's chambers.

Joey looped his arm around Stacey. He couldn't say anything. He couldn't even think because of all the turmoil inside him. Cameron had surprised him, that was for sure.

"What do we do now?" Stacey asked as she

bounced Rachel.

"We pray. For us and for Cameron."

CHAPTER TWENTY

AFTER A CELEBRATORY dinner, Stacey and Joey walked in their home together, a sense of peace stealing over them. Stacey put Rachel to bed, taking extra care to enjoy the evening's outcome, knowing for at least a little while longer, Rachel was still hers. Her thoughts were also with Cameron, who had made such a selfless decision and was no doubt in a huge amount of pain tonight without the possibility of her daughter being in her arms soon. Despite Stacey's worries about Rachel's safety, Cameron had proven she had it in her to be a good mother. She hoped one day Cameron could be a part of Rachel's life.

Which brought her mind to rest on another subject. When Rachel was older, would she feel rejected by Cameron? She saw it all the time on the television and read about it in books. Adopted children often felt abandoned, but what about kids who have two loving parents and one just didn't happen to be biological? Would Rachel ever resent Stacey as her mother or wish Cameron was the one in her life rather than her?

No doubt, it would happen. Probably during the ornery teenage years when Rachel was exploring who she was and what her life meant to her. But she resolved to herself as Rachel shoved her thumb in her mouth that she would be the best mother, no matter how angry Rachel might be one day over her circumstances. Stacey would do the right thing and love her enough to get them through the tough times.

Quietly slipping out of the room, Stacey made her way back to the living room where Joey sat on the couch, staring at his hands.

"She's sound asleep," Stacey said, sitting next to him and taking his hand in hers.

"I keep wondering how Cameron is feeling tonight. She's gotta be having a hard time."

"Whatever she's doing, I'm sure she feels like she did the right thing. She was brave, and she'll realize it soon enough."

Joey looked at her, the sorrow clear in his eyes. "I just wish she would have made better choices so things were different."

Stacey studied their hands together, watching Joey's thumb trace lazy circles against her skin. "I can't say I regret anything she did. Maybe I do for Rachel's sake, but if she had been the model mom, I wouldn't be where I am right now."

Silence filled the room. Finally Joey shuffled on the couch until he faced her. "My speech in the courtroom…it's what you've been trying to tell me all along. Everything is about choices."

Hope soared within Stacey. Did he finally understand?

"I was reading my Bible the other day and came across some verses that kind of summed it all up for me. It was my light bulb moment."

"What verses?"

Joey moved and grabbed her Bible off the table in front of them and turned directly to a bookmarked page. He cleared his throat. "Love is patient. Love is kind. Love does not envy. Love does not boast. Love is not proud or rude. Love isn't selfish or quick tempered. It doesn't keep a record of wrongs others do. Love rejoices in truth, not evil. Love is always supportive, loyal, hopeful, and trusting. Love never fails."

Tears were in Stacey's eyes. It wasn't until

he looked at her that she saw the brightness in his eyes.

He cleared his throat again. "There's nothing in there that says love is a feeling."

"No, there's not." Still she waited before launching into a speech. She wanted to see if his conclusion was the same as hers.

"When we first got married, I kept thinking the way I felt about you was so different than what I felt for Cameron. At first maybe I thought I could never get past our friendship. Then I thought I didn't love Cameron because I never knew her like I know you." He linked their hands together, bringing her knuckles up to kiss them one at a time.

"I know you love me, Joey," she whispered.

"No you don't. You've lived in doubt for months now. I can say it until I'm blue in the face, but the doubt will always be there until you realize I understand what love is now."

"What is it? Tell me."

With a grin, he said, "Keeping with the theme of the day, love is a choice. You chose to risk never having true love for the possibility of it. You loved me more than yourself. You loved our daughter more than yourself. You've stayed humble about it, too. When I needed space to think about my relationship with Cameron, you gave it to me. And when I messed up and hurt you, you forgave me. You've never once turned your back on me. You've never failed me. You love me in the truest sense of the word."

"I do love you, Joey," she said as a tear slipped down her cheek.

"Well, today I've made a choice. I'm going to love you, too. In every way I'm supposed to. Those feelings I thought I would never have suddenly appeared the second I realized it wasn't intended to be a feeling. Feelings are great, don't get me wrong, but I was waiting for something superficial. Something that fades with time for everyone. It's what you were trying to tell me. That one day, we won't tremble every time we touch. One day, one of us, God forbid, could be in a nursing home or a coma, or whatever…and nothing would change. Our love for each other would still be a choice, every day. And even though I enjoy seeing you naked and get a warm fuzzy every time you're holding Rachel, the love I have for you stems from something much deeper, something I can't even put words to."

"I know how you feel, Joey." Her heart pounded in her chest and tears had free reign on her cheeks. Tenderly, he wiped them away.

"You do. Thank you for loving me. Thank you for loving Rachel. And thank you for being my wife. I'm luckiest man on earth," he whispered, kissing the last of her tears away.

"I think so, too," Stacey said with a sniff and then giggled.

He laughed. Then his face turned serious and he leaned in, kissing her deeply. Telling her without words how much she meant. He cherished her in his kiss, worshiped her. When he pulled away slightly, he smiled.

"You know, I do enjoy feeling occasionally, too. And boy do you make me feel…"

At a loss for words, she kissed him again, making it clear she wanted more. But she pushed him away, studying his face, reveling in the moment.

"What are you thinking?" he asked, worry etched on his brow.

"I'm thinking little mousy Stacey Ingram McCrary just landed the hot next door neighbor for life."

Joey threw his head back and let out a bark of laughter. "I'd say you're right. And I hope you choose to let me stay and love you the rest of my life."

"We'll see what we can work out."

In a show of flexing muscle and strength, Joey scooped her up and carried her to the bedroom, where they spent the whole night in each other arms.

ABOUT THE AUTHOR

Stephanie Taylor is a freelance editor, author and business owner. She spends her time making other authors' dreams come true at Astraea Press as Editor in Chief and Owner. Stephanie opened Astraea Press because of the lack of non-erotic book publishers and has finally found a home for her books.

Stephanie has a doctorate in multi-tasking and can actually walk a tight rope while balancing a dinner plate on her head and typing her next novel with the other. She lives in Alabama with her three children and her wonderful husband of eleven years.